THE BIG **BIG** **BIG** **BOOK** OF

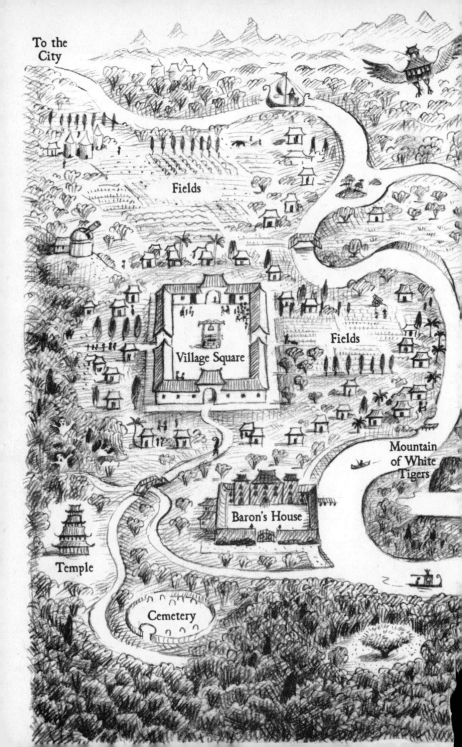

To the
City

Fields

Fields

Village Square

Mountain
of White
Tigers

Baron's House

Temple

Cemetery

THE BIG **BIG BIG BOOK** OF

Tashi

written by
Anna Fienberg and
Barbara Fienberg
illustrated by **Kim Gamble**

ALLEN&UNWIN

Allen & Unwin
83 Alexander Street
Crows Nest NSW 2065
Australia
Phone: (61 2) 8425 0100
Fax: (61 2) 9906 2218
Email: info@allenandunwin.com
Web: www.allenandunwin.com

Cataloguing-in-Publication details are available
from the National Library of Australia
www.librariesaustralia.nla.gov.au

ISBN 978 1 86508 563 0

Cover illustration by Kim Gamble
Cover and text design by Sandra Nobes
Set in Sabon by Tou-Can Design

This book was printed in June 2011 at
McPherson's Printing Group
76 Nelson Street, Maryborough, Victoria 3465, Australia
www.mcphersonsprinting.com.au

15 14

My mother, Barbara, always read stories to me
when I was little. At bedtime we'd travel to all the
secret places in the world, through books.

We both make up our own stories now,
and Tashi began when Barbara was telling me how,
when she was a child, she used to tell whoppers.
Creative fibs. Tall stories. And kids would crowd
around, dying to hear the latest tale. We talked
about a character like her—someone who told
fantastic stories—and over many cups
of tea we cooked up Tashi.

ANNA FIENBERG

Anna Fienberg is a storyteller with a special talent
for fantasy and things magical. Kim Gamble is one
of Australia's leading illustrators for children.
For ten years they have been working together to
produce such wonderful books as *The Magnificent
Nose and Other Marvels*, *The Hottest Boy Who
Ever Lived*, the *Tashi* series, the *Minton*
picture books, and *Joseph*.

Contents

Tashi

written by
**Anna
Fienberg**

and

**Barbara
Fienberg**

•

illustrated by
Kim Gamble

'I have a new friend,' said Jack one night
at dinner.
'Oh, good,' said Mum. 'What's his name?'
'Tashi, and he comes from a place very far
away.'

3

'That's interesting,' said Dad.

'Yes,' said Jack. 'He came here on a swan.'

'A black or white swan?' asked Dad.

'It doesn't *matter*,' said Jack. 'You always ask the wrong questions!'

'How did Tashi get here on a swan then?' asked Mum.

'Well,' said Jack, 'it was like this. Tashi's parents were very poor. They wanted to come to this country, but they didn't have enough money for the air fare. So they had to sell Tashi to a war lord to buy the tickets.'

'How much did the tickets cost?' asked Dad.

'It doesn't *matter,*' said Jack. 'You always ask
the wrong questions!'

'So why is Tashi here, and not with the war
lord?' asked Mum.

'Well,' said Jack, 'it was like this. Soon after Tashi's mother and father left, he was crying for them down by a lake. A swan heard his cries and told him to jump on his back. The swan flew many days and nights until he arrived here, right at the front door of Tashi's parents' new house.'

'Did he arrive in the morning or the afternoon?'
asked Dad.

'It doesn't *matter,*' said Jack. 'And I'm not
telling you any more because
I'm going to bed.'

A week passed and Jack ate lunch with Tashi
every day. And every day he heard a marvellous
adventure.

He heard about the time Tashi found a ring at
the bottom of a pond, and when he put it on his
finger he became invisible.

He heard about the time Tashi met a little woman as small as a cricket, and she told him the future.

And he heard about the time Tashi said he wanted a friend just like Jack, and look! the fairy had granted his wish.

But at the end of the week he heard the best
adventure of all.

'Listen to what happened to Tashi yesterday,'
Jack said to Mum and Dad at dinner.
'Last night there was a knock at Tashi's door
and when he opened it, guess who was standing
there!'

'Who?' asked Mum.

'The war lord, come to take Tashi back! Tashi turned and ran through the house and out the back door into the garden. He hid under the wings of the swan.'

'Go on,' said Mum.

'Well, the angry war lord chased him out into
the night and when he found the swan he
shouted, "Where did young Tashi go?"

'The swan answered, "If you want to find
Tashi, you must go down to the pond. Drop
this pebble into the water, and when the ripples
are gone you will see where Tashi is hiding."'

'Did the war lord find the pond?' asked Mum.
'Well,' said Jack, 'it was like this. The war lord
did as the swan told him and dropped the
pebble into the pond. But when the water was
still again, he didn't see Tashi. Instead he saw
his own country, and his own palace, and he
saw all his enemies surrounding it, preparing to
attack.

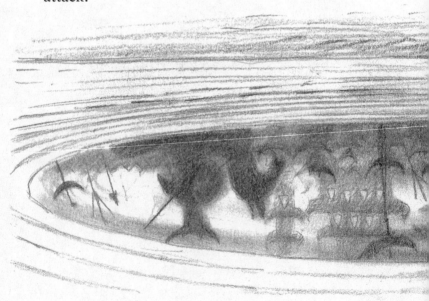

'The war lord was very upset by what he'd seen in the pond and he said to the swan, "I must go home at once!"

'"I will take you," said the swan. "Just climb on my back." And bending his head under his wing he whispered, "Goodbye Tashi, I am homesick for my country. Just stay in the long grass, and he won't see you. Goodbye."'

'Can I bring Tashi home tomorrow to play?'
asked Jack.

'Oh, yes,' said Mum and Dad. 'We're dying to
meet Tashi.'

Jack and Tashi sat at the kitchen table, drinking their juice.

'Would you like to play in the garden now?' asked Mum.

'Oh, yes!' said Tashi. 'I like gardens.'

'We could look for a dragon to kill,' Jack said
hopefully to Tashi.

'Are there any dragons left in the garden?'
asked Dad.

'You *always* say the wrong thing!' said Jack.

'He's right though,' said Tashi as they closed the door behind them. 'There aren't any dragons left in the whole world. Can you guess how I know?'

'How?' asked Jack.

'Well, it was like this. Come and I'll tell you about the time I tricked the last dragon of all.'

DRAGON BREATH

Jack took Tashi outside to the peppercorn tree.
They climbed up to Jack's special branch and
when they were sitting comfortably, Jack said,
'Did you really meet a dragon?'

'Yes,' said Tashi, 'it was like this. One day Grandmother asked me to go to the river to catch some fish for dinner.'

'Was this in your old country?' asked Jack.

'Of course,' said Tashi. 'Grandmother doesn't believe in travel. Anyway, before I set off, Grandmother warned me, "Whatever you do, Tashi," she said, "don't go near the steep, crumbly bank at the bend of the river. The edge could give way and you could fall in. And," she added, "keep your eyes open for dragons."'

'*Dragons!*' said Jack. 'What do you do if you meet a dragon?'

'Well, it was like this,' said Tashi. 'I walked across the field to the river and I caught five fish for dinner. I was just putting them into a couple of buckets of water to keep them fresh when I saw a cloud of smoke. It was rising from a cave, further up the mountain.'

'Ooah, did you run away home?' asked Jack.
'Not me,' said Tashi. 'I took my buckets and
climbed up the mountain and there, sitting at
the mouth of the cave, was the biggest dragon
I'd ever seen.'

'Have you seen many?' asked Jack.

'I've seen a few in my time,' said Tashi. 'But not
so close. And *this* dragon made me very cross.

39

He was chomping away at a crispy, dragon-breath-roasted pig.

'"That's my father's pig you're eating," I said.

'"I don't care," said the dragon. "I needed something to cheer me up."

'"You can't eat other people's pigs just because you feel like it," I told him.

'"Yes, I can. That's what dragons do."

'So I sat down next to him and said, "Why do you need cheering up?"

'"Because I'm lonely," said the dragon. "There was a time when I had a huge noisy family. We'd spend the days swooping over the countryside, scaring the villagers out of their wits, stealing pigs and geese and grandfathers, and roasting them with our dragon breath.

Then we'd sing and roar all night till the sun
came up. Oh, those were the days!" The dragon
sighed then and I moved back a bit. "But Mum
and Dad grew old and died, and I ate up the
rest of the family. So now I'm the only dragon
left."

'He looked straight at me and his scaly dragon eyes grew slitty and smoky. "A few mouthfuls of little boy might make me feel better," he said.'

'Oh no!' said Jack. 'What happened then?'
'Well, it was like this. I quickly stood up, ready to run, and the water in my buckets slopped out over the side.

'"Look out!" cried the dragon. "Watch your step! Dragons don't like water, you know. We have to be careful of our fire."'

'*Aha!*' said Jack.

'Yes,' said Tashi. 'That gave me an idea. So I looked him in the eye and said, "You're not the last dragon, oh no you're not! I saw one only this morning down by the river. Come, I'll show you, it's just by the bend."

'Well, the dragon grew all hot with excitement and he followed me down the mountain to the bend in the river. And there it was all steep and crumbly.

'"He can't be here," said the dragon, looking around. "Dragons don't go into rivers."
'"This one does," I said. "Just look over the edge and you'll see him."

'The dragon leaned over and peered down into
the water. And he saw another dragon!
He breathed a great flaming breath. And the
other dragon breathed a great flaming breath.

He waved his huge scaly wing. And the other dragon waved his huge scaly wing.

'And then the steep crumbly bank gave way and *whoosh!* the dragon slid *splash!* into the river.

'An enormous dragon-shaped cloud of steam rose up from the river, and the water sizzled as the dragon's fire was swallowed up.'

'Hurray!' cried Jack. 'And *then* did you run away home?'

'Yes,' said Tashi. 'I certainly did run home because I was late. And sure enough Grandmother said, "Well, you took your time catching those fish today, Tashi."'

'So that's the end of the story,' said Jack sadly.
'And now all the village was safe and no-one
had to worry any more.'

'Well, it wasn't quite like that,' said Tashi. 'You see, the dragon had just one friend. It was Chintu the giant, and he was as big as two houses put together.'

'*Oho!*' said Jack. 'And Chintu is for tomorrow, right?'

'Right!' said Tashi.

And the two boys slipped down from the tree
and wandered back into the house.

Tashi
and the
GIANTS

written by
Anna Fienberg

and

Barbara Fienberg

·

illustrated by
Kim Gamble

Jack ran all the way to school on Tuesday
morning. He was so early, the streets were
empty. Good. That meant he would have plenty
of time to hear Tashi's new story.

Tashi was Jack's new friend. He'd come from a
land far away, where he'd met fire-breathing
dragons and fearsome warlords. Today, Tashi
had promised the story of Chintu, the giant.

Tashi was waiting for Jack on a seat by the
cricket pitch.

'So,' said Jack, when he'd stopped puffing and
they were sitting comfortably. 'Did you really
meet a giant, Tashi?'

'Yes,' said Tashi. 'It was like this. Do you remember how I tricked the dragon, and put out his fire? Well, the dragon was furious, and he flew to the castle where his friend Chintu the giant lived. The dragon told him what I had done and Chintu boomed:

"*Fee fie fo fum*
I'll catch that boy for you, by gum!"

'Chintu took one of his giant steps over to our village and hurled down great boulders, just as if they were bowling balls. Third Uncle's house was squashed flat as a fritter. Then the giant roared, "Bring Tashi out to me."

'The giant was quiet for a moment. Then he
answered, "If you don't bring Tashi to me, I
will come back in the morning and crush every
house in the village."

71

'The people all gathered in the square to discuss what to do. Some wanted to take me to the giant's house that night. Others were braver and said I should run away. While they were still arguing, I took the lantern and set out for Chintu's castle.

'I walked and walked until finally, there before me was the giant's castle, towering up to the sky. One path led up to a great door and windows filled with light, but another led down some winding stone steps.

'I took the lower path but the steps were so high I had to jump from each one as if they were small cliffs. After a while I spied an arched wooden door. It wasn't locked and I pushed it open. It gave a groaning creak and a voice called out, "Who's there? Is that you, Chintu, you fly-bitten lump of cowardly husband?" 'Now I saw a big stone-floored room and right

in the middle was an enormous cage. Inside the cage was another giant.'

'Ooh!' said Jack. 'Two giants! Didn't you want to run?'

'No,' said Tashi. 'Not me. See, it was like this. The giant in the cage was sitting at a table eating some noodles. She was terrible to look at. She had only four teeth, yellow as sandstone, and the gaps in between were as big as caves.

'Well, while I was staring at her she said in a huge voice, "Who are you?"

'So I told her that I was Tashi and what had happened and that I had come to persuade Chintu not to kill me. She gave a laugh like thunder and said, "You won't change his mind easily, it sets like concrete. I should know, he is my husband! He tricked me into this cage and locked me up, all because we had an argument about the best way to make dumplings. He likes to grind bones for them, but I say flour is much better. Now Tashi, you need me to help you."'

'And she needed you to help *her*!' Jack said
excitedly.

'Right,' said Tashi. 'So when she pointed to the
keys over on a stool, I reached up and dragged
them over to her. Mrs Chintu snatched them
up and turned one in the lock. "Now I'll show
that lumbering worms-for-brains Chintu who
is the cleverer of us two!"

'As she walked past, I scrambled up her skirts and hung on to her belt. She picked up a mighty club that was standing by the door and then she tip-toed to some stairs that led up and up through the middle of the castle.

'We came to a vast hall and there he was,
sitting on a bench like a mountain bent in the
middle. He was staring into the fire, bellowing
a horrible song:

> "Fee fie fo foy,
>
> Tomorrow I'll go and get that boy,
>
> No matter if he's dead or jumping
>
> I'll grind his bones to make my dumpling."

'Mrs Chintu crept up behind him, grabbed his tufty hair in one hand and held up the club with the other. I slid down her back to the floor.

'"Chintu, you pig-headed grump of a husband, I can escape from your cages, *and* I make the best dumplings. Will you admit now that I am more than a match for you?"

'The giant rolled his great eyes and caught sight of me. "Who is that?" he roared.

'"That is the boy who chops our wood." And Mrs Chintu winked at me. "Now, let the boy decide who makes the best dumplings." She let go of Chintu's hair and gave me a hard look.
'"Very well," Chintu said, and he rubbed his huge hands together.

'Later, they put some sacks down on the floor for me to sleep on. As he was going to bed, Chintu whispered—it was like a thunderclap in my ear—"If you decide that *her* dumplings are better, your bones will make my next batch."

And as his wife went by, she said, "If you decide that *his* dumplings are better, I'll chop you up for my next pot of soup."

'All night I walked up and down the stone
floor, thinking what to do. And then I had one
of my cunning ideas. I crept downstairs to the
kitchen and had a good look about.'

'What were you looking for, Tashi?' asked Jack.

'Well,' said Tashi, 'it was like this. The next morning Mrs Chintu boiled her dumplings and then Chintu boiled his. When the dumplings were cooked they both spooned up one each, as big as footballs.

'"We must put a blindfold on the boy so he doesn't know which dumpling he is eating," said Mrs Chintu, and her husband tied a handkerchief over my eyes.

'I took a bite of one dumpling and swallowed it slowly. Then I tried the other. They watched me fiercely.

'When I had finished I said, "These are the best dumplings I ever tasted, and they are exactly the same."

'"No they're not!" thundered Chintu.

'"Taste them yourself and see," I said.

'So they did and they were very surprised.
"The boy is right. They *are* the same," said
Mrs Chintu. "And they are the best dumplings
I ever tasted."

'So then I told them, "That's because I went
downstairs to the kitchen last night and I
mixed the ground bones and the flour together.
That's what makes the best dumplings—bones
and flour."

'"What a clever Tashi," cried Mrs Chintu.

'"Oho! So that's who you are," bellowed
Chintu, and he scooped me up in his great red
hands. "I promised my friend the dragon that I
would serve you up to him in a tasty fritter the
next time he came to breakfast."

'"Maybe so," said his wife, "but just try
another dumpling first."

'The giant did, and when he had finished he
thought for a minute. It was the longest minute
of my life. Then the giant sighed and licked
his lips. "Dragon can have a plate of these
dumplings instead," he said. "They are
exquisite. Be off with you now, Tashi."

'And so this time I walked out the great front door, as bold as you please. When I returned to the village they were still arguing about whether to give me up to Chintu or to let me run away. "I don't have to do either!" I cried, and I told them what had happened.

'"What a clever Tashi!" cried Grandmother.'

'So that's the end of the story,' said Jack sadly. 'And everyone was safe and happy again.'

'Yes,' said Tashi, 'that is, until the bandits arrived.'

THE BANDITS

One night Jack was reading a book with his father.

'This story reminds me of the time Tashi was captured by some bandits,' said Jack.

'Oh good, another Tashi story,' said Dad. 'I suppose Tashi finished up as the Bandit Chief.' 'No, he didn't,' said Jack. 'It was like this. One wet and windy night a band of robbers rode into Tashi's village. They were looking for some shelter for the night.

'But next morning, just as they were leaving, the wife of the Bandit Chief saw Tashi. He reminded her of her son, who had sailed away on a pirate ship, and she said to her husband, "That boy looks just like our son, Mo Chi. Let's take him with us."

'So Tashi was picked up and thrown on to one
of the horses and away they went. He sneaked
a good look about him, but he was surrounded
by bandits, and it was impossible to escape. So
Tashi had to think up one of his cunning plans.

'The first night when the bandits were still sitting around the fire after their dinner, the Bandit Chief said to Tashi, "Come, boy, sing us a song as Mo Chi did, of treasure and pirates and fish that shine like coins in the sea."

'Tashi saw that this was his chance. So what do you think he did?'

'Sang like a nightingale,' said Dad.
'Wrong!' said Jack. 'He sang like a crow. The bandits all covered their ears and the Bandit Wife said, "Stop, stop! You sing like a crow.

You had better come over here and brush my hair like my son used to do." Tashi bowed politely but as he stepped around the fire, he filled the brush with thistles and burrs so that soon her hair was full of tangles.

'"Stop, stop!" cried the Bandit Wife, and her husband told her, "This boy is not like our son. He sings like a crow and he tangles your hair." Tashi put on a sorrowful face. "I will do better tomorrow," he promised.

'"You'd better," whispered the Chief's brother,
Me Too, "or I'll boil you in snake oil."

'The next day when the bandits moved camp, they put all the rice into three big bags and gave them to Tashi to carry. When they came to a river, what do you think Tashi did?'

'Well,' said Dad, scratching his chin, 'he's such a clever boy, I expect he carried them over one by one, holding them up high.'

'Wrong!' said Jack. 'He dropped them all into the river. The bandits roared with rage. They called to Tashi to mind the horses. Then they jumped into the water and tried to recover the bags of rice that were sinking further down the river.'

'But Tashi reached them first, I suppose,'
said Dad.

'No, he didn't,' said Jack, 'and when the
bandits came back, all angry and dripping,
they found that he had lost all the horses. The
robbers began to whisper about the Bandit
Wife, and Me Too gave Tashi evil looks. It
took them a whole day to find the horses
again.

'Well, that night, the Bandit Chief said to his wife, "This boy is not like our son. He sings like a crow, he tangles your hair, he loses the rice and scatters the horses." Tashi put on a sorrowful face. "I will do better tomorrow," he promised.

'"You'd better," whispered Me Too, "or I'll pluck out your nose hairs, one by one."

'On the third day, the bandits decided to attack the village where another band of robbers were staying. Just before dawn they quietly surrounded the camp—and what do you think Tashi did then?'

'He rode into the village and captured the chief,' guessed Dad.

'Wrong!' cried Jack. 'They were just preparing to attack, when Tashi accidentally let off his gun.

'The enemy was warned and Tashi's bandits had to gallop away for their lives.

When they were at a safe distance they stopped. The Chief's brother wanted to punish Tashi—he said he'd tie him up and smother him in honey and let man-eating ants loose upon him—but the Bandit Wife said, "No, let him come back to camp with me. He can help me roast the ducks we stole yesterday and we will have a feast ready for you when you return."

'So she and Tashi worked all day, plucking, chopping and turning the ducks on the spit, and mouth-watering smells greeted the bandits as they drew near the camp that evening. And what do you think Tashi did then?'

'Washed his hands for dinner,' said Dad.

'Wrong!' said Jack. 'Just as the robbers jumped down from their horses, Tashi stumbled and knocked a big pot of cold water over the almost-cooked ducks and put out the fire.

'"Enough!" shouted the Bandit Chief to his wife. "This boy is not like our son. He sings like a crow, he tangles your hair, he loses the rice, he scatters the horses, he warns our enemies—and now he has spoilt our dinner. This is too much." And he turned to Tashi.

"You must go home to your village now, Tashi. You are a clumsy, useless boy with no more brain than the ducks you ruined."

'Tashi smiled inside, but he put on a sorrowful face and turned to the Bandit Wife. "I'm sorry that I wasn't like your son," he said, but she was already on her way down to the river to fetch some more water.

'Tashi turned to go when a rough hand pulled him back.

'"You don't deserve to go free, Duck Spoiler," snarled Me Too. "Say goodbye to this world and hullo to the next because I'm going to make an end of you."

'But as he turned to pick up his deadly nose-hair plucker, Tashi shook himself free and tore off into the forest. He could hear the bandit crashing through the trees after him, but if he could just make it to the river, he thought he would have a chance.

'He was almost there when he heard a splash.
He looked up to see the Bandit Wife had
slipped on a stone and had fallen into the water.

'"Help!" she cried when she saw Tashi. "Help me, I can't swim!"

'Tashi hesitated. He could ignore her, and dive in and swim away. But he couldn't leave her to drown, even though she was a bandit. So he swam over to her and pulled her ashore.

'By now all the bandits were lined up along
the bank and the Chief ran up to Tashi.
"Thank you, Tashi. I take back all those hard
words I said about you. Fate did send you to
us after all."

'Me Too groaned and gnashed his teeth.

'"Brother," said the Bandit Chief, "you can see Tashi safely home."

'"Oh no, thanks," said Tashi quickly, "I know the way," and he nipped off up the bank of the river, quicker than the wind.'

'So,' said Dad sadly, 'that's the end of the story and Tashi arrived safely back at his village.'

'Wrong!' said Jack. 'He did arrive back at the village and there were great celebrations. But at the end of the night, when everyone was going sleepily to bed, Third Uncle noticed that a ghost-light was shining in the forest.'

'And that's another Tashi story, I'll bet!'
cried Dad.

'Right!' said Jack. 'But we'll save it for dinner
when Mum gets home.'

Tashi

and the
GHOSTS

written by
**Anna
Fienberg**

and

**Barbara
Fienberg**
•

illustrated by
Kim Gamble

125

'Guess what Tashi is having for dinner
tonight,' said Jack, as he spooned up the
last strawberry.

127

'Roast leg of lion caught fresh from the jungle,' Jack's father said keenly.
'Wrong!' Jack laughed.

'Grilled tail of snake caught fresh from the desert,' his mother said proudly.
'Double wrong! He's having Ghost Pie, from a special recipe that he learned from—'

'Ghosts!' cried Mum and Dad together.
'Right!' said Jack. 'And would you like to
know how he came by this spooky recipe?'
'Yes indeed,' said Mum.

'Can't wait,' said Dad, getting comfortable
on the sofa. 'So tell us. After Tashi tricked
those giants and teased the bandits, how did
he meet these *ghosts*?'

'Well, it was like this,' said Jack. 'The very night that Tashi escaped from the bandits' camp and ran home to his village, Third Uncle saw a ghost light shining in the forest.'

'What does a ghost light look like? How would I know if I saw one?' asked Mum nervously.

'Like a street lamp, without the post?'
guessed Dad.

Jack shook his head. 'No, Tashi said it was
more like a small moon, sending out rays of
light into the trees, like white spider threads.'

'Ooh, can you get tangled up in them?'
shivered Mum.

'In a way,' said Jack. 'Ghost monsters can
be sticky, and they tend to hang around,
Tashi says. Well, the next night there were
more ghost lights. They came closer, and
closer, and Tashi called his parents to see.
Soon the news spread through the village
and everyone was peeping behind their
curtains at the phantom lights flitting
through the forest.

'In the morning the people hurried to the
square to talk about the ghosts. Some
wanted to pack their belongings and move
right away. Others wanted to burn down
the forest so the ghosts would have no
place to live. Finally they decided to ask
Wise-As-An-Owl what he thought would
be the best plan.'

'*My* plan would be to ignore them,' said
Dad. 'If the ghosts got no attention, they'd
probably go away.'

'I don't think that works with ghosts, Dad,'
said Jack. 'Anyway, Wise-As-An-Owl told
the men to organise a great beating of
saucepan lids outside their houses that night
as soon as it grew dark. They did, and sure
enough, the ghosts slipped away, back into
the forest.

'But the next night the ghosts came back. They drifted up like smoke, nearer and nearer, until they were pressing their faces against the windows. Their mouths were huge and gluey, and the air in the houses began to grow stale and thin as they sucked at the keyholes and under the doors. Everybody in the village burst out into the streets, coughing and choking. Men and women thundered around making a great crashing noise with saucepans and garbage lids and firecrackers. The ghosts melted away but Tashi was sure that they weren't gone for long.'

'They'd have gone forever if people had ignored them,' muttered Dad. 'Who comes back for no attention?'

'Well,' continued Jack, 'in the morning Tashi went to see his father's Younger Brother. He lives up on a hill overlooking the village and spends his nights studying the stars through a great telescope that he built years ago.

'Tashi told him about the ghost monsters who were frightening the villagers and he cried, "Of course, I know why they have come now. Look, Tashi," and he took out his charts of the stars and his Book of Calculations. "You see, look here. In three days' time there will be an eclipse of the moon."'

'I'll bet Tashi didn't know what *that* was,' Dad laughed. He was already looking for the dictionary.

'Yes,' said Jack patiently. 'It's what happens when the moon is blacked out for a while by the shadow of the earth. Well, Younger Brother said to Tashi, "Last time there was an eclipse, the river flooded and your father's pigs were drowned. And the time before that we had a plague of locusts that ate the village fields bare. You'll see, with this next eclipse there will be a haunting of ghosts."

'At that, Tashi thought "*Aha!*", and he
began to form one of his cunning plans.
He waited two more days and sure enough
the saucepan lids did no good at all. Each
night after the people went to bed, the
ghosts floated back to the village. On the
third night, a brave dog rushed out of his
house but as he drew breath to bark, he
sucked in a tendril of grey ghost, and it was
terrible to see. He choked and gasped and
his fine black coat grew pale and wispy until
he was just a shadow, melting into the
stones.

'The villagers drew their curtains against the
sight of it, but Tashi crept out into the
forest. At first he could see only the small
moons of light, tangling amongst the leaves.
But as he tip-toed into the dark heart of the
forest, he saw the ghosts themselves.

'And there were hundreds of them—
hopping ghosts, prowling ghosts, gliding
ghosts. They were like white dripping
shadows, fat and thin, tall and tiny,
whipping all around him.

'Suddenly Tashi felt a cold weight on his head. "Oh no, a jumping ghost," he thought, and he tried to pull it off. But it slid down over his eyes and nose like sticky egg white, and he could hardly see or breathe. "Oh no, a jumping *and* slithering ghost," he groaned, as it trickled down his back and clamped his arms.

'"Let me go!" Tashi screamed, and as he screamed he sucked in a bit of cold eggy ghost. He felt as if he were choking, and then more and more ghosts pressed their bodies against him. Like thickening fog they crowded around and Tashi didn't want to breathe for fear of sucking in those damp whirling phantoms.

'And then a huge glowing ghost as big as a ship loomed over him. Its eyes were empty, and it was the meanest-looking ghost Tashi had ever seen.'

'Has Tashi seen many ghosts before this?' asked Dad.

'Yes, he's seen a few in his time, he says. Well, this mean-looking, leader ghost asked Tashi why he had come into the forest at night.

'"I've come to warn you," Tashi hissed at him, blowing out wisps of ghost as he spoke. "If you don't leave our village at once, you will all suffer."

'The huge ghost laughed. The sound rippled like wind through the forest. "And how exactly will we suffer?"

'"Well," Tashi told him, "my friend the Red-Whiskered Dragon-Ghost will come and punish you if you hurt me or frighten the people in my village."

'There was a low buzz as the ghosts swarmed together, discussing Tashi's news. The smaller ghosts were trembling, and their outlines were fading a little with fear. But the leader ghost was scornful. "Why should we believe *you*? No one could hurt *us*!"

'"Oh, I can easily prove it," Tashi said. "Just look at the moon up there. See how round and full it is? Now I will call my friend, the Red-Whiskered Dragon-Ghost, and he will open his huge jaws and eat the moon right up. When the moonlight disappears you will know how great he is and you will be afraid."

'Tashi called out into the night, "O mighty Red-Whiskered Dragon-Ghost, when I count to three, please open your jaws and take your first gigantic bite out of the moon!"

'Tashi counted *o-n-e* very, very slowly. He was worrying, deep inside himself—what if Younger Brother was wrong with his calculations? Could an eclipse be late?

'He counted *t-w-o* even more slowly. Was
the moon shrinking a little?

'"Are you ready, ghost monsters?" Tashi
cried, and then he shouted, "*THREE!*" just
as the black shadow of the earth moved
across the moon and sliced off a great piece.

'The ghosts watched as the moon grew smaller and smaller until there was not even a needlepoint of light in the dark sky. The moon had been swallowed up.

'The ghosts moaned with fear and their sighs blew through the trees like a gale of ice. "Please," they cried to Tashi, "tell your friend to give us back the moon. Tell him to spit it out again!"

'Tashi was silent for a moment, letting the ghosts feel the awful weight of a sky without light. Their own little moons of ghost-light were paler now, swamped by the darkness of the night.

'"All right," Tashi said finally, "I will ask him to grant you your wish—if you do two things. First, you must all leave this part of the earth, and never come back. Every now and again, the Red-Whiskered Dragon-Ghost will gobble up the moon for a short time, just to remind you never to frighten my village and its people again."

'"Very well," the leader ghost grudgingly agreed. "And the second thing?"
'"You must give me the recipe for Ghost Pie. I have heard that it is delicious, and for three days after eating it a person can walk through solid walls."

'The ghost leader let out a roar of rage. The little ghosts quivered and faded into the trees. They were shrinking with every moment, hanging like cloudy raindrops from the forest leaves.

'"Ghost Pie is one of our greatest secrets," the leader ghost spat. He waved for some of the older ghosts to come closer. They whispered together and then the leader ghost turned to Tashi. "We will do as you say, young Tashi, if you promise never to reveal the ingredients to any other *living* soul."'

'Aha!' cried Dad, slapping his knee. 'So when are we going to have a taste of pie?'

'Tashi says we can all come over to dinner next Saturday to try it, as long as we don't ask any questions about how it is made,' said Jack.

'It's a promise,' beamed Dad. He stood up and stretched. 'Oh well,' he said, 'I suppose that's the end of the story, and Tashi's had no more trouble with ghosts then.'

'That's right,' smiled Jack, 'but only one
moon went by before he was in a sticky
situation with a truly wicked Baron!'

THE MOUNTAIN OF WHITE TIGERS

The doorbell rang.

'I'll go,' Jack called, because he knew who it would be. Tashi was spending the day with him, and they were going for a ferry ride. Jack had said to come early, in time for breakfast.

But when Tashi walked in, Mum peered at his face with a worried frown. 'You look a bit pale this morning, Tashi,' she said. 'Yes, I know,' sighed Tashi. I've been up burping Ghost Pie all night.'

'Pancakes coming!' cried Dad from the kitchen.
Tashi turned a little paler.

When they were all sitting around the table in the garden, and Tashi had managed three pancakes after all, Jack decided that he'd waited long enough. 'How did you meet this Wicked Baron?'

'Well, it was like this,' said Tashi. 'One day I went to visit Li Tam, my favourite auntie. I always like going to her place because she has the most interesting house in the village. The rooms are all decorated with painted scrolls and she lets me touch the delicate bowls and vases and hand-carved swords.'

'Does Li Tam do a lot of sword-fighting?'
asked Dad.

Jack rolled his eyes, but Tashi just smiled.
'No, the swords belonged to her father.
Anyway,' he went on, 'this particular day I
didn't even get a chance to knock on the
door, when it was flung open and out
stormed Li Tam's landlord, the wicked
Baron.'

'Aha!' cried Mum and Dad.

'Yes, he was grinding his gold teeth, and he pushed me out of the way. I picked myself up and as I dusted my pants off, I wondered why the Baron looked so angry.'

'Was he a friend of Li Tam's?' asked Dad.

'Oh no!' said Tashi. 'He was no one's friend. The only thing he loved was gold. You see, this Baron had once been poor, but he had tricked an old banker out of his riches, and then he had stolen some money here and hired a few pirates there, until he had a huge fortune.'

'Where did he keep all his gold?' asked Mum.

'Well, it was a great mystery,' said Tashi. 'The people in the village were certain that he had hidden it away in a deep cave. But no one could be quite sure because the cave lay at the top of The Mountain of White Tigers.'

'I've never seen a white tiger,' said Dad, 'but I've heard they are the fiercest kind.'

'Yes,' said Tashi. 'Anyway, Li Tam was very
upset after the Baron stormed out. She told
me that he had called to tell her that she
would have to leave her home at once
because he had been offered a good price
for it. And Li Tam had cried out, "Why
must you have *my* house? You own the
whole village!" But the Baron had ordered
her to pack her bags by the end of the week.

'"Look at this then!" Li Tam had told him, and she'd pulled a piece of paper from the hidden drawer in her cupboard. On it was written a promise from the old banker that she could stay in the house for as long as she pleased.

'The Baron's face had grown red and that is why he'd stormed out, knocking me over as he went. But Li Tam was worried. "Tashi," she said to me, "I just know he won't stop at this. He'll try to find a way to push me out of my home."

'And sure enough, the next day when I went
to visit her, I found the house was alive with
mice. And they were everywhere. All the
tables and chairs, shelves and cupboards
seemed to be moving, crawling with
wriggling bodies. From under beds, inside
wardrobes, came loud squeals and
scratchings. Well, Li Tam ran to me and
said, "Look what the Baron has done! He
sent his servants during the night to tip
sacks of mice in through the windows."

'"Don't worry, Auntie," I said, "I will fix it." I ran home for a bag of rice cakes. I crumbled them up and laid a trail of crumbs from Li Tam's house right up to the Baron's kitchen door. The mice scrambled after me, gobbling up the crumbs as they went. And soon it was the *Baron* who had a houseful of mice.

'He was furious—roaring like a bull with a bellyache!—and when he saw the villagers laughing at him behind their hands, he charged right into the square on market day and shouted to them, "Tomorrow is the day you pay your rent money. From now on, all your rent will be three times as much as before. Be sure to have the money ready!" The people were shocked. "What will we do?" they wailed. "We have nothing more to give!"

'When I ran to tell Li Tam she said, "Oh,
Tashi, if only we had the money to buy our
own houses, then we would never have to
worry about the wicked Baron again."'
'Aha!' cried Mum and Dad and Jack
together.

'Aha!' agreed Tashi. 'That's when I felt one
of my clever ideas coming on. So that night,
when the last light went out, I crept through
the streets to the Baron's house and tapped
on the kitchen window. Third Aunt, who
was the Baron's cook, opened the door.

'"Auntie, please let me in," I whispered. I
ran over to the table where I'd often sat on
baking mornings and pulled away the rug
that lay under it. There was a little door
over a flight of steps leading down into
darkness.

'"You can't go down there, Tashi," said
Third Aunt. "That passage leads all the way
to the Mountain of White Tigers, and no
one has ever returned from there."
'"The Baron must have," I said, "so I
expect I will manage it, too." Still, as I
peered into the blackness below, I did feel
just a little afraid.'

'I don't wonder,' shivered Dad. 'Sometimes I
feel a little afraid just going to put the
garbage out at night.'

'Well,' said Tashi, 'I stopped looking into the dark and I whispered, "Hand me your lamp, please, Auntie. I'll be back before the Baron comes down to his breakfast in the morning."

'The passage twisted and turned, winding like a rabbit's burrow deep into the earth. I held my lamp high, but I could only see a short way in front of me, and the blackness ahead looked like the end of the world.

'I must admit that once or twice I did think of going back. I had no idea how long I'd been walking, or how much time I had left.

'But at last I felt the ground slope upwards,
and I could feel my heart start thumping
hard as I climbed up the steep path—and
suddenly, at the top, I stopped. The path
was blocked. I held up my lamp and saw a
door, with a gold latch. I pulled at it and
whoosh!—the door swung open.

'I stepped out onto the Mountain of White Tigers.

'My face tingled in the snowy air and I looked nervously into the night. The lamp showed me a path, but on each side of it were tall black trees, and behind those trees who knew *what* was waiting!

'But I couldn't bear to go back empty-handed. And just then, I heard a growl, deep as thunder. I peered into the dark, but I could see nothing, only hear a grinding of teeth, like stones scraping. The growling became roaring, and my ears were ringing with the noise, and then, right in front of me, a white shape came out from behind a tree, and then another and another. The tigers were coming!

'They came so close to me that I could see their whiskers, silver in the moonlight, and their great red eyes, glowing like fires. They were even fiercer than I had been told, and their teeth were even sharper in their dark wet mouths, but I was ready for them. Second Aunt had warned me that the one thing white tigers fear is fire.

'I took a big breath and swung my bright burning lamp round and around my head. I charged down the path roaring, "Aargh! Aargh!" till my lungs were bursting.

'The tigers stopped and stared at me. They must have thought I was a whirling demon, with circles of light streaking about their heads. They bared their teeth, growling like drums rolling. But I saw them flinch, their white coats shivering over their muscles, and slowly, one by one, they turned away, gliding back through the trees. Oh, I was so happy watching those white shapes disappearing! I ran on and there, looming up above me, was the mouth of the cave.

'The entrance was blocked by a huge stone boulder. I tried to squeeze through but the gap was too small.'

'Did you have to turn back then, Tashi?'
Jack held his breath.

'I thought for a moment I'd have to,' Tashi
nodded. 'But then I remembered that I'd
popped a piece of Ghost Pie into my pocket
before leaving home. I quickly nibbled a bit
and pushed at the boulder again. This time
my hand slid right through it and the rest of
me followed as easily as stepping through
shadows.

'I ran inside *whooping*! There were sacks and sacks of shiny, golden coins! Puffing and panting, I loaded them into a huge knapsack I had with me, and hauled it onto my back to carry.'

'I wish *I'd* been there to help you!' Jack said
wistfully.

'Me too,' said Tashi. 'That knapsack made
my knees buckle. And then, coming out of
the cave, I had to whirl my lamp round my
head and roar as well, just in case there
were still tigers lurking in the trees.'
'So how did you crawl back through the
tunnel with all that gold on your back?'
asked Mum.

'Well, it was like this,' said Tashi. 'I took the sack off my back and put it on the ground. Then I rolled it along with my feet. It was easier that way, but very slow. And of course I was getting very worried about the time.

'I crept back up the stairs and into the kitchen as it was growing light. Third Aunt was just putting a match to the kitchen fire, and she almost dropped the poker when she saw me.

'"What a clever Tashi," she cried, when she spied the gold.

'Well, I thanked her, but I wasn't finished yet, oh no! I crept to each house in the village and whispered a few words, passing a little sack of gold through the windows.

'Next morning all the people were in the square when the Wicked Baron arrived for his rent. Wise-As-An-Owl stepped forward. "Baron," he began, "our children who went away to other parts for work have done well and sent gold home to their families. Now we would like to buy our houses."

'And all the villagers stepped up and poured the gold onto the table before the Baron. What a sight it was! The mountain of coins glittered so brightly in the morning sun that I had to turn my eyes away! But The Baron stared. He couldn't *stop* looking! Still, he was hesitating. He liked getting money every month from his rents, but he couldn't resist the sight of all those shining, winking coins. "Very well," he agreed, and I could tell he was itching to gather up the coins and run his fingers through them. "I'll sign right now," and he took the papers that Wise-As-An-Owl had ready for him.

'That night there was a great feast with music and dancing to celebrate the new freedom of the village. My grandmother and Second Aunt were singing so loudly, that only I heard the faint bellow of rage coming from the Mountain of White Tigers.'

'Oh well,' said Dad, 'that wicked Baron got what he deserved, eh, Tashi? And I suppose all the village people were happy and contented from that day on.'

'Oh yes,' agreed Tashi, 'and so was I, until I came face to face with the Genie. But now we'd better go—if we don't run all the way we'll miss the ferry! Are you coming, Jack?' And the two boys raced out the door, as if the Genie itself were after them.

Tashi

and the
GENIE

written by
Anna
Fienberg

and

Barbara Fienberg

·

illustrated by
Kim Gamble

Jack and Tashi ran up the wharf and
hurtled onto the ferry. They flung themselves
down on a seat outside, just as the boat
chugged off.

Tashi watched the white water foam behind
them. The sun was warm and gentle on
their faces. Jack closed his eyes.

'What a magical day!' they heard a woman say as she brushed past them. Jack's eyes snapped open.

'Talking of magic,' he said to Tashi, 'let's hear about the time you saw that genie. What did he look like? How did you meet him?'

'Well,' said Tashi, taking a breath of sea air,
'it was like this. One day, not long before I
came to this country, I was in the shed
looking for some nails. Grandmother called
me, saying she wanted a few eggs. I
gathered about four or five from under the
hens and then looked around for a dish to
put them in. I spied an old, cracked one on
a top shelf, covered with a dirty piece of
carpet. But there was something very
strange about this bowl.'
'Ooh,' squealed Jack.
'I know, I know
what was in it!'

'Yes,' nodded Tashi. 'When I lifted the carpet I saw a bubbling grey mist inside; soft rumbling snores were coming from it. The snores turned to a splutter when I poked it. A voice groaned, "Oh not again! Not already!" And the mist swirled and rose up in the air. Two big sleepy eyes squinted down at me. "And only twenty-five years and ten minutes since my last master let me go!" it said. Well, I was *very* excited.'

'Who *wouldn't* be,' Jack agreed.

'"You're a genie!" I shouted.

'"What if I am?" said he.

'"Why aren't you in a bottle?" I asked. "Or
a lamp, like normal genies?"

'The genie looked shifty. "Oh, my master
went off in too much of a hurry to put me
back in my lamp. So I just crept into this
bowl, hoping for some peace and quiet."'

Tashi winked at Jack. 'I happened to know a lot about genies, because my grandmother was always telling me what to do if I met one. So I looked him in the eye and said, "Now that I've found you, don't you have to grant me three wishes?"'

'The genie groaned. "Wishes, wishes! People don't realise they are usually better off leaving things the way they are." But he pulled himself up to his full height and straightened his turban. "What is your command, master?" he bowed.

'I thought for a moment. "I would like an enormous sack of gold." Imagine, I could build a splendid palace, for all my family to live in.

'The genie snapped his fingers and—
TA RA—a sack of gold lay at my feet! I ran my hands through the glittering coins and held one up. Hmm, before I build the palace, I thought, I might just run down to the sweet-maker's shop.'

'Good idea!' cried Jack. 'You could buy a *million* sweets, to last you till you're a hundred and ten!'

'Yes, but when Second Cousin at the shop took my coin, she looked at it carefully and rubbed it on her sleeve. The gold rubbed right off. "This coin is no good, Tashi," she told me. "It's only copper."

'I stamped back to the shed and angrily shook the genie out of his dish. "Those coins are only copper!" I shouted.

'The genie yawned. "Really? All of them? How tragic." He stretched. "Maybe a few at the bottom will be gold. What I need now is a glass of tea before I do any more work."'

'What a lousy, lazy genie!' exploded Jack.
'Yes,' agreed Tashi. 'And it gets worse. By
the time I'd brought his tea, I'd thought of
my second wish. "What about a flying
carpet?" I asked. Oh, if only I'd known.
The genie looked at me doubtfully. "Flying
carpets are not my best thing," he said. But
I was firm with him, so he snapped his
fingers, and there, floating at my knees, was
a glittering carpet. It was the most
magnificent thing I had ever seen. All
smooth and polished as skin, it was
patterned with hundreds of tiny peacocks,
with eyes glowing like jewels.

'The carpet trembled as I climbed on. The genie showed me how to tug at the corners to steer it. And then we were off, the carpet and I, out of the shed, over the house and across the village square. All the people were amazed, as they looked up and saw me waving at them.'

'I bet they were!' cried Jack. 'My dad would have fainted with shock. So, did you get to see Africa? Or Spain?'

'No,' Tashi frowned. 'It was like this. I had
just turned in the direction of Africa, in fact,
when the carpet suddenly dipped and
bucked like a wild horse. My knees slipped
right to the edge! I threw myself face down
on the carpet, grabbing hold of the fringe.

'The carpet heaved up and down, and side to side, trying to throw me off. A hundred times it kicked me in the belly, but I clung on. The world was swirling around me like soup in a pot, and then I saw we were heading straight for the willow tree beside my house. I came crashing down through the branches. When I got my breath back, I marched off to find the genie.

'"Well, you certainly aren't very good at your job, are you?" I scolded as I brushed the leaves from my hair.'

'Is that all you could say?' yelled Jack. 'I would have called him a fumble-bumble *beetle*-brain at the very least.'

'Yes, but I still wanted my third wish,' Tashi sighed. 'Oh, if only I'd known. Well, the genie just yawned at me and said, "What is your third—and last—wish, master?"

'I thought carefully. One thing I had often longed for was to meet Uncle Tiki Pu, my father's Younger Brother. He had run away to the city while he was still a boy, but my father had told me stories of his pranks and jokes. "Yes, that's it!" I said. "I would like to meet my Uncle Tiki Pu."

'It was suddenly very quiet in the shed. The genie rose up and clicked his fingers. Nothing happened. "You will find him in your bedroom," said the genie, and slithered back into his bowl. I ran to my bedroom and there was my uncle, stretched out on my bed.

'"Ah, Tashi," he said, "it's about time
someone came to find me. My life has been
very hard in the city." Before I could say
that I was sorry to hear it, and how pleased
the family would be to have him back home
again, Uncle Tiki Pu went on. "This bed
is very hard, however."

'I looked around the room. "Where will *I*
sleep, Uncle?"

'"Who knows?" he answered in a bored voice. "Get me something to eat, Tashi, a little roast duck and ginger will do. And tell your mother when she comes home that these clothes need washing."

'He pointed to a pile of his clothes beside my toy box. The lid was open and inside my box were jars of hair oil and tins of tobacco instead of my train set and kite and rock collection.

'"Where are my things?" I cried.

'"Oh, I threw them out the window," he told me. "How else could I make room for my belongings?"

'I ran outside and gathered up my toys. Two wheels had fallen off my little red train. "What about *my* belongings?" I called through the window.

'"Don't worry about them," replied Uncle
Tiki Pu. "You won't be living here much
longer. This house is too small for all of us
now that I've come back. You can have my
old job in the city, Tashi. But mind you take
a rug to sleep on because they don't give
you any bedding there, and the stony
ground is crawling with giant spiders that
bite. See, I've got the wounds to prove it."

'And he lifted his holey old singlet to show
big red lumps all over his tummy, like
cherry tomatoes.

'"Do they give you food in the city?" I
could hardly bear to ask.
'"No, there's never enough, so you have to
hunt for it. That's where the spiders come in
handy. If you squish them first, they're not
bad in a fritter. Oh, and watch out for
alligators—they swim in the drains. Well,
goodbye and good luck! You'll need it, ha
ha!" And he laughed a wicked laugh.'

Tashi stopped for a moment, because he
couldn't help shivering at the terrible
memory of his uncle, and also because Jack
was jumping up and down on his seat in
outrage. The woman who had said 'What a
magical day!' was staring.

'I know,' said Tashi. 'I know, I couldn't
believe it either, that a member of my family
could be so evil. My head was pounding,
and I ran straight to see the genie.'
'How could *he* help, that old *beetle*-brain?'

'Well,' said Tashi. 'It was like this. I picked
up his bowl and tried to wake the genie
again. I shook him and begged him to get
rid of Uncle Tiki Pu, but he just closed his
eyes tightly and said, "Go away, Tashi.
You've had your three wishes and that's
that." Suddenly I put the bowl
down and smiled. I had just
had a cunning idea. I
remembered another thing
Grandmother always
told me about genies.

'I hurried back to my room and said to Uncle Tiki Pu, "You are quite right. This house is very small and poky. How would you like to live in a palace instead?"

'Uncle Tiki Pu sat up with a bounce. "Just what I've always wanted!" he cried. "How did you *know*?"

'"Come with me," I told him, "and I will show you how to do it."

'I opened the door of the shed and led him to the genie's bowl. Uncle let out a howl of joy when he saw what was curled up inside, but when the genie rose into the air, his eyes weren't sleepy any more. They were bright and sly.

'"I am your new master, so listen carefully, Genie," Uncle Tiki Pu began. "For my first wish—"

'The genie interrupted him. "There will be
no wishes for you, my friend. You really
should have been more careful. Don't you
know that every seventh time a genie is
disturbed, *he* becomes the master, and the
one who wakes him must be the slave?"
He glided over and arranged himself on
Uncle Tiki Pu's shoulders. "Take me to
the city," he commanded, "and be quick
about it."

'Uncle Tiki Pu's face was bulging with rage
and his knees sagged, but he staggered out
of the shed with his load. As he sailed past,
the genie turned and gave me a big wink.
'"Look out for alligators!" I called.'

Jack was quiet for a moment, thinking. He watched people stand up and stretch as the ferry slowed, nearing the city.

'I hope nothing with teeth lives in *our* drains,' he said. 'Well, Tashi, that's amazing! Did you really fly on a magic carpet?'

For an answer, Tashi opened the top buttons
of his jacket, showing Jack the gold coin
hanging on a cord around his neck. 'How
else would I have this?' he said.

And the two boys stepped off the ferry and
strolled over to the ice-cream stand at the
end of the wharf.

TASHI AND THE STOLEN CHILDREN

Jack burst into the kitchen. 'Tashi's back!' he cried.

'Oh, good,' said Dad. 'Has he been away?'
'Yes, I *told* you,' said Jack, 'don't you remember? He went back to the old country to see his grandmother for the New Year holiday. And while he was there, something terrible happened.'

'His grandmother ran away with the circus?' suggested Dad.

'No,' said Jack. 'She can't juggle. But listen, you know the war lord who came looking for Tashi last year?'

'Yes, I do remember him,' said Dad. 'He was the only war lord in Wilson Street last summer, so I won't forget him in a hurry.'

'Yes, and guess what,' Jack began, but Mum interrupted him.

'Come and have some afternoon tea, while you tell us,' she said, and brought a tray into the living room.

'Well,' said Jack, when they were settled comfortably. 'It was like this. When Tashi arrived back in his village, it was all quiet. *Strangely* quiet. None of his old friends

were playing in the square, and he could
hear someone crying. His grandfather told
him that the war lord had just made a raid
through the village. He'd captured nearly all
the young men for his army—and he had
kidnapped six children as well!'

'What did he take the *children* for?'
asked Mum.

'So that the men would fight bravely and
not run away home,' Jack told her. 'If they
didn't fight, he was going to punish
the children.'

'He deserves to be fried in a fritter, that war
lord!' exploded Dad.

'Yes,' agreed Jack. 'Well, just then the Wan twins came running back into the village square,

'They had hidden while the soldiers seized the young men. Then they'd followed the war party to see where their uncles were being taken.

'The twins said that the children had been put in the dungeon of the war lord's palace. The twins searched and climbed and tapped and dug, but they could find no way in. They said the children were lost forever.

'Everybody in the square listened to the
Wan twins' story, and a dreadful moaning
began. The sound of sadness rose and
swelled like a wave. Parents and aunties and
cousins hung onto each other as if they were
drowning. Then, one by one, people turned
to Tashi. He had once worked for the war
lord in that very palace.'

'Uh oh,' Dad shook his head. 'I bet he was wishing that he had gone on holidays another time.'

'Not Tashi,' said Jack. 'He slipped away to think, and when he returned he went to his grandfather's box of firecrackers and filled his pockets. Then he set off for the palace of the war lord.

By evening, he reached the field where the soldiers were camped.

'He crept past the guards and found the
uncles. They were miserable, sitting silent
and cold, far from the cooking fires. Tashi
whispered to them that they must get ready
to leave at any moment, as he was on his
way to the dungeon. One man clung to him,
crying, "My little sister is only five years
old, Tashi. She will be so frightened. You
must find the children." Tashi promised to
be back by morning.

'Then he went on alone. He remembered a
secret passage into the palace that he'd
discovered when he was living there before.
You entered in a cave nearby and came out
through a wardrobe in the war lord's very
own bedroom.'

'Ugh,' shuddered Mum. 'I'd rather be
anywhere in the world than *there*.'
'I know,' shivered Dad. 'A man like that,
you can imagine how his socks smell.'

'Well, anyway,' Jack went on, 'Tashi found
the cave and pulled aside the bushes
covering the entrance. He ran through the
damp tunnel and held his breath as he
pushed at the wardrobe door. It creaked.
What if the war lord had just come upstairs
to get a sharper sword?'

'Or change his socks?' put in Dad.

'Tashi held his breath. He peeped around
the door. The room was empty. He tiptoed
out into the hall and down the stairs. At the
last step he stopped. He felt the firecrackers
in his pockets, and quivered. A daring plan
had popped into his head. But, he
wondered, was he brave enough to do it?

'Instead of going further down the stairs into the dungeon, he found his way along to the kitchens. The cooks were busy preparing a grand dinner for the war lord and didn't notice Tashi as he crawled behind the oil jars and around the rice bins.'

'What was he doing?' asked Mum.

'Having a little snack, of course,' said Dad, taking a bite of Jack's scone.

'You'll find out if you pay attention,' said Jack, and he moved his scone to the other hand. 'When Tashi left the kitchen he could hear the cries of the children, and the sound of their sobbing led him down to the dungeon. Two guards were talking outside the dark, barred room where the children were held. Tashi hopped into an empty barrel close by and called out in a great loud voice, *"The war lord is a beetle-brain!"*'

'*NO!*' cried Mum and Dad together.

'*YES!*' crowed Jack. 'The guards jumped as if they'd just sat on a nest of soldier ants. "One of those pesky children has managed to get out!" the fat guard hissed. "Then we'd better catch him," said the other, "before the war lord boils us in spider sauce."

'As soon as they ran off, Tashi turned the big key they had left in the lock and opened the dungeon door.

'The children recognised Tashi and crowded around, telling him all that had happened. "Shush," whispered Tashi, "wait till we get outside. The danger isn't over yet."

'He led them quickly up the stairs and through the long hallways until at last they came to the great wooden front door of the palace. Tashi reached up and pulled on the big brass latch. The door swung open and the children whooped with joy. They streamed out, falling over each other in their hurry. Tashi picked up the littlest one and set him on his feet. "Home we go!" he cried.

'But no. Just then a huge hand reached
down and plucked Tashi up by the collar.
He was face to face with the furious war
lord. Their noses almost touched. The
war lord's skin was rough, like sandpaper.

"*RUN!*" Tashi called to the children. "Run
to your uncles down by the camp!"

'The war lord shook Tashi, as if he were a
scrap of dirty washing. His iron knuckles
bit into Tashi's neck. He breathed fish and
grease into Tashi's face. "So, you foolish
boy," he growled. "You have come back.
You won't escape again. Look well at the
daylight outside, for this is the last time
you'll see it. You'll work in the dungeons
from now on."

'Tashi thought of the mean black bars on the window of the dungeon. Only a cockroach could stay alive in there. His eyes began to water and he started to sniff.

'"Scared, are you?" the war lord jeered.
'"No, I can smell something," said Tashi, "can't you?"'
'Socks!' cried Dad.

'The war lord sniffed. The air *did* seem rather smoky. Suddenly there was a loud explosion and they heard feet pounding over the stone floor. "Fire!" shouted the war lord, and he dropped Tashi and ran off towards the noise, calling for the guards to follow him.

'Tashi sped down the steps and soon found the children and their uncles. They were waiting for him over the hill, beyond the camp. From there they had a good view of the palace.

'It was blazing fiercely—the windows were red with the glow of fire inside, and a great grey cloud of smoke climbed above it.

'"Weren't we lucky the fire started just then!" said the littlest boy. His brother laughed and looked at Tashi. "I don't think luck had anything to do with it," he said.

'"Well," said Tashi modestly, "as a matter of fact I did empty the gunpowder out of my firecrackers and laid a trail up to the kitchen stove. I hoped we would manage to get out before it reached the ovens. It blew up just in time."

'"What a clever Tashi!" the children yelled, and the uncles hoisted him up onto their shoulders and they sang and danced all the way home.

'Phew!' said Dad. 'That was a close shave. I suppose Tashi could relax after that, and enjoy the rest of his holiday. Did he have good weather?'

'Yes, at first,' said Jack, 'until the witch,
Baba Yaga, blew in on the winds of a
dreadful storm.'

'Baba Yaga?' said Dad nervously. 'Who is she?'

'Oh, just a witch whose favourite meal is
baked children. But Tashi will tell us all about
that. What's for dinner tonight, Mum?'

Tashi

and the
BABA YAGA

written by
**Anna
Fienberg**

and

Barbara Fienberg

•

illustrated by
Kim Gamble

JACK'S DAD SAT up in bed reading the newspaper. He had a cold, and his tissue box was nearly empty. '"Beach Houses For Sale",' Dad read aloud. 'How would you like to move to a house near the beach, Jack?' He blew his nose. 'Just imagine—an early morning swim, watching the sun rise over the sea. Look at this one—a nice little wooden house, with plenty of personality.'

251

'Looks as big as a beehive to me,' said Jack.
'Anyway, I like it *here*—near all my friends.
Besides,' Jack narrowed his eyes and tapped
the side of his nose slyly, 'you've got to be
careful about exploring new houses. You
never know what you may find inside.'

Dad put down his paper. 'Really?' He
smoothed a place on the bed for Jack to come
and sit down. He rubbed his hands together.
Yes, he could definitely feel a story coming
on—one of Jack's Tashi stories, no doubt.
Since young Tashi had moved into the
neighbourhood, and become best friends with
Jack, they'd heard some amazing adventures.

'I suppose your friend Tashi knows all about new houses?' said Dad.

'Yes, when he was back in the old country, a new house did arrive in his village one day.'

'Arrive?' repeated Dad, puzzled. 'How could a house *arrive*? No, wait a second. MUM,' called Dad, 'MU-UM, come and listen to a story!' He grinned at Jack. 'She'd be so cross if she missed out.'

Mum came panting into the room, her arms full of dirty washing. She plonked it on the floor and curled up next to Dad.

'Wacko!' she cried. She glanced scornfully at the washing. 'That can wait. So, what's it all about?'

'Well, it was like this,' Jack began, and he shivered as he remembered Tashi's words of last night. 'Baba Yaga blew in to Tashi's village on the winds of a terrible storm.'

'Baba Yaga? Who is that?' coughed Dad. 'Someone looking for a new house?'

'Pay attention and you'll find out,' said Jack.

'And don't breathe on me,' said Mum.

'Well, one night, when Tashi was quite small, stinging rains lashed the village and wild winds blew washing off the lines and chickens out of their nests. Branches were torn from the trees and whole houses were whisked miles away.

'The next morning, when Tashi walked
along the road, he saw people scurrying
about trying to find lost belongings that had
been scattered far and wide. He offered to
help and, going further and further from the
village, he found cooking pots and slippers
high up in the trees.

'Because he was looking up, he almost
stepped on a raven that was pinned under a
fallen branch. Tashi gently lifted the bird
from the leaves and twigs and placed it on a
grassy mound. The bird was very weak and
thirsty so Tashi gave it a drink of water
from his bottle.

'"Thank you," said the raven. "You have
been my friend. Maybe one day *I* will be
able to help *you*."'

'Ho *ho*,' crowed Dad, and blew his nose like a trumpet.

'Well,' Jack went on, 'as Tashi walked on through the forest, he came upon a house in a clearing where there had been no house before. And what an extraordinary house it was! It stood on scaly yellow chicken legs, and the claws dug deep into the earth. Above, a thread of crooked smoke rose out of a crooked chimney.'

'Hmm!' Dad wrinkled his nose. 'Just like the newspaper said—a nice little wooden house with plenty of personality!'

'Ugh! Did Tashi dare to peep inside?' asked Mum.

'Well,' said Jack, 'it was like this. He put down all his bundles and crept closer. He wanted to see more, but was a bit afraid. And then, suddenly, the door opened and an old woman stepped outside.

'"Aha, our first visitor has arrived, Alenka," she crowed to a young girl who came to the window. "Won't you come in and tell us all about yourself while you have a glass of tea?"

'Tashi hesitated for a moment, but he was
so eager to explore this weird house that he
thanked her and followed her inside.

'There was an enormous stove in one
corner of the room and nearby, on a stool,
lay a half-plucked goose. Sticky feathers and
smears of blood covered the young girl's
hands.

'As he sipped his tea, Tashi asked the old woman how it was that her house had appeared so suddenly in the forest. The old woman leaned towards Tashi and looked into his face. "My name is Baba Yaga," she rasped, "and I come from a land far, far away. The storm blew me right over the mountains, into this forest. But I don't think I'll stay here. It seems a dismal sort of place to me, not many children about." Her voice scraped like sandpaper on wood. Her black eyes pierced Tashi's own. Then she reached over and pinched his arm. "You look a nice juicy boy however, and if there's one thing I do enjoy, it's Boy-Baked-In-A-Pie."

'Tashi could hardly believe his ears; did she really mean it, or was she just teasing?'

'Probably just teasing,' Dad said heartily. Then he looked at Jack's face and gulped. 'Wasn't she?'

'Go on, Jack,' said Mum. 'What happened next?'

'Well,' said Jack, 'it was like this. Tashi was staring at her, half-smiling and hoping she was joking, when suddenly she smiled back. He gasped in horror. Her teeth were made of iron!

'He looked around wildly and saw, through the window, that the sun had vanished behind the clouds. The fence posts glowed white against the dark sky. Tashi peered closer. His heart thumped and he bit his lip, hard. On top of each post sat a small skull—a child's-size skull—with a candle lit inside it. "Wah!" he screamed.

'Baba Yaga leapt up. "Take the boy," she
roared at her daughter, "and get him ready
for baking. We'll have a fine meal tonight!"
And she hobbled out into the forest to
gather some herbs and mushrooms.

'Alenka dragged Tashi over to the oven. Her strong fingers bit down through his jacket like claws. With one hand she built up the fire, then dropped Tashi onto the oven spade, as if he were nothing but a loaf of bread.

'Quick, he thought, what can I do? He gazed longingly through the open door, and spied an old apple tree. *Aha!* His heart leapt with hope.

'"Don't you use apples and spice when you roast m-meat?" he asked. "Everyone in my village says that it makes a dish much tastier."

'"Does it now?" said Alenka. "I'll try it then."

'And she strode out of the room and down
the steps to gather some apples in her
apron, bolting the door behind her.

'Quick as lightning, Tashi pulled off his jacket and trousers and shoes and put them on the goose that was left lying on the stool in the corner. He stood back for a second to look. Wasn't something missing? Of course: the goose-boy needed some hair.

'*Hurry hurry*, yes, that would do. He snatched up a black sock that Alenka had been knitting and unravelled some wool. When he had arranged it with the curl over the goose's "face", it looked so real that Tashi felt a bit sick. He just had time to hide in the cupboard before Alenka came back.

'"That was a good idea of yours, Tashi,"
she said as she stuck some cloves in the
apples. She pushed one apple up each leg
and arm of the goose-boy's trousers and
jacket, and then slid the oven spade right
into the red heart of the oven.

'Inside his cupboard, Tashi trembled. He heard the oven door slam, and soon the smell of cooking crept in through the cracks of the wooden cupboard.

'When Baba Yaga came back, she scolded Alenka for not waiting for the mushrooms. '"Great greedy gizzards, why don't you do as I tell you? Boy-Baked-In-A-Pie needs mushrooms, and *you* need your brains boiled!"

'But the old woman stopped finding fault when she sniffed the delicious smells coming from the oven.

'"Apples and cloves," Alenka announced proudly. "Tashi told me how to do it."

'They sat down at the table and began to eat. Baba Yaga chewed on a small piece of leg, and smacked her lips. "This dinner is quite tasty," she said grudgingly. She paused a moment.'

'For a burp, I bet,' said Dad. 'A woman like that would have no manners.'

'Tashi didn't mention any burping,' replied Jack. 'Anyway, *then* the old woman began to look suspiciously at the meat. She poked it with her fork. "This looks like goose." She paused again. "It smells like goose. It *is* goose!"

'The old woman stood up and pointed her craggy finger at Alenka. "You stupid, snail-witted lump! Can't you do anything right? Now where did that Tashi get to? You stay here and search the house while I see if he ran to the village."

'Alenka got down on her hands and knees and looked under the bed. She looked behind the screen and then she turned towards the cupboard. Through the crack in the door, Tashi could see her moving towards him. He began to shake. In the tight, dark space of the cupboard he could hardly breathe.

'But then he saw something else. There, across the room, sitting on the windowsill was his friend, the raven.

'"Are you looking for something?" the bird called.

'"Yes," said Alenka. "A juicy boy that was supposed to have been our dinner."

'"Ah," nodded the raven. "I saw such a boy hiding in the garden just now."

'"Good!" Alenka shouted, and she ran down the steps to catch Tashi.

'Quickly Tashi slipped out of the cupboard.
He whispered, "Thank you!" to the raven
as he clambered out the window. Then he
ran through the forest, with the trees
moaning in the wind and the storm clouds
racing across the sky and a rusty old voice
calling on the air like a crow at dusk.

'The next morning Tashi's mother was very cross that he had lost all his clothes. When Tashi told her that Baba Yaga had cooked them, thinking he was inside them, she didn't quite believe him.

'"Come, I'll show you," said Tashi, and he led her into the forest. The strange house was still there, standing on its bony old chicken feet. And the crooked smoke was still drifting out of the crooked chimney.

'Tashi's mother shivered, and drew him close to her. "What did I tell you?" said Tashi.

'But just then, while they were both still
staring, the house rose up high on its legs
and scurried out of the forest, flying over
the mountains and away, never to be seen in
Tashi's village again.'

Jack's parents were silent for a moment, thinking. Then Dad sneezed.

'Ugh!' he shivered. 'I hope that house doesn't blow anywhere near *here*. No one would want a place like that, even if they were selling it for chicken feed.'

Jack leapt off the bed with a grin. 'Funny you should mention *chickens*, Dad, because they were the cause of Tashi's next problem.'

'Well, the worst thing about chickens is chicken poo,' said Dad. 'That might be a smelly problem, but how could it be *dangerous*?'

'You'll see this afternoon,' Jack called over
his shoulder as he ran out of the room.
'Tashi's coming over and he'll tell you
himself!'
'Is it the afternoon yet?' asked Dad, who
didn't know what time it was since he'd
been in bed.
'No, not for hours,' Jack called back.
Dad groaned, and flopped back on the
pillow.

GONE!

At four o'clock Jack met Tashi at the
garden gate.

'Sorry I'm late,' panted Tashi, 'but three of
our chickens escaped through a hole in the
fence and we had to chase them to the creek
and back. Pesky things!'

Tashi wiped his feet on the mat. Jack looked
down curiously at Tashi's boots, and sniffed.

'Perhaps I'd better leave them outside,' said
Tashi.

'Perhaps,' agreed Jack.

'So,' said Jack, when they were sitting comfortably, 'did you get all three chickens back?'

'Oh yes,' said Tashi, 'but I remember a time when it wasn't so easy. Once, every hen in our village disappeared. Nothing was left behind—not even a feather floating in the air.'

'How dreadful,' said Mum, coming into the room. 'What did you do for eggs?'

'Well,' said Tashi, stretching out his legs, 'it was like this.'

'Wait,' cried Jack. 'Dad's still asleep. Fair's fair.' He scrambled upstairs, flung open his father's door, and shouted 'BABA YAGA!' Dad screamed and shot out of bed as if the witch was swooping through the window right behind him.

He was still breathing heavily when he was settled on the sofa with a rug over his knees. He stared at Tashi. 'I don't know how you could even look at chickens again after Baba Yaga,' he said, and sneezed.

'Hmm,' Tashi nodded, 'but a man has to eat. When all the hens disappeared, no one in the village had a clue where they could be. People were grizzling because they had to start work without their omelettes. They invented excuses to poke about in each other's houses, but they found nothing.

'One day my mother threw down her spoon
and said she was tired of trying to cook
without eggs. She sent me over to Third
Aunt, who worked as a cook for the wicked
Baron. Since he was the richest man in the
village, she thought that perhaps he might
have a few eggs left.'

'Oh I remember *him*!' cried Dad. 'He was that rascal who kept all his money on a mountain—'

'Guarded by a pack of white tigers,' shuddered Mum.

'Yes,' agreed Tashi. 'He had the heart of a robber, and the smile of a snake, and I didn't like going near him. But what else could I do? I set off at once and on the way I met Cousin Wu. He had just returned from a trip to the city, and he couldn't stop talking about the wonders he'd seen there. "The best thing of all," he said, "was the Flying Fireball Circus. You should have seen it, Tashi—the jugglers and the acrobats on the high trapeze—I couldn't believe my eyes."

'"You are lucky, Wu," I sighed. "I don't suppose we will ever see a circus here. The village would never have enough money to pay for one to visit."

'We walked along in silence for a while, and then I asked Cousin Wu if he wanted to come with me to the Baron's house. Suddenly he seemed to be in a great hurry to visit his sister, so we said goodbye and I went on my way.

'Unfortunately, just as I was opening the
gate to the Baron's house, the wicked man
himself leant out the window and saw me.
"Be off with you, you little worm," he
shouted. "I don't want to see you hanging
about my house!"'

'Worm—*he's* the worm,' said Dad crossly.
'Someone ought to squish him!'

'Well,' Tashi went on, 'I pretended to run off home, but as soon as the Baron closed his shutters, I ducked back into the kitchen where Third Aunt had made some delicious sticky sweet rice cakes, my favourite. When I had wolfed down five or six, I remembered the eggs.

'"Of course you can have some," said Third Aunt. "We have plenty. More than we know what to do with, in fact."

'"Have you?" I said. "That's very interesting." And I followed her outside to an enormous shed and waited while she unlocked the door. And do you know what? I found hundreds of hens—and some of them were my old friends! I recognised Gong Gong's Pullet and Second Cousin's big Peking Red.

'"Don't wait for me," I told Third Aunt.
"I'll fill this bowl and be out in a minute."
When she left, I walked amongst the birds
and made sure that all the village hens were
there in the Baron's chicken house. Then I
sniffed the smell of cigars. Strange, I
thought. Cigar smoke in a chicken house? I
sniffed again and the skin on my neck
tingled. Slowly I turned around. And there,
in the doorway blocking the light, stood the
wicked Baron.

'He marched inside and closed the door
behind him. "So, little worms wriggle into
peculiar places," he said with a nasty sneer.
"But can they wriggle out again, I wonder?"

'"You have stolen all our chickens!" I cried.
"Why? Whatever are you going to do with
them?"

'"That is none of your business…but then, maybe I'll tell you since you won't be here long enough to do anything about it." And he grinned, showing all his glinting gold teeth. "I am going to sell half of them to the River Pirate, who'll be sailing past this house at midnight. Then tomorrow, I'll be able to charge whatever I like for my eggs because no one else will have any to sell. I'll make a fortune! Golden eggs, they'll be! What do you think of that, little worm?"

'I stared at him. It was hard to believe anyone could be so mean.'

'I know,' agreed Dad, nodding his head. 'The newspapers are full of crooks getting away with it. Makes your blood boil.'

'Well, I was determined *he* wouldn't get away with it. I edged toward the door. "You can't keep me here," I told him, thinking I could make a dash for it.

'The Baron laughed fiercely. It sounded like a growl. "Oh no, little fish bait, I have plans for you. I will lock you up in the storeroom until midnight, when the River Pirate will take *you* as well as the hens. A pirate's prisoner, that's what you'll be!" And he grabbed me and threw me over his shoulder like a bit of old rope, and dropped me into the cold, dark storeroom.

'At first, there was just darkness, and silence. But as my eyes grew used to the gloom, I saw the walls were thick stone, and a square of grey light shone in through one small high window. I felt all round the heavy iron door, but it was padlocked, as tight as a treasure chest. I bent down to study the floor, to see if there were any trapdoors, or loose stones. And it was then that I saw it. Lying in the corner, curled up like a wisp of smoke, was a white tiger.'

'The Baron's tiger!' screamed Jack. 'What did you do?'

'Well, it was like this. I just stayed where I was and made no sound. I could see that its eyes were closed. Its legs twitched now and then, as if it were chasing something in a dream. It was asleep, but for how long? I put my head in my hands. There was no way out. I felt like a fly in a web. Only *my* web was made of solid stone.

'If only I had my magic ghost cakes, I thought. I could walk through that wall, as easily as walking through air. I searched in my empty pockets. Wait! There was a small crumb. But would it be enough to get me all the way through those thick walls? Should I take the chance?'

'Yes, yes!' cried Jack.

Tashi nodded. 'I put the crumb on my tongue and as I swallowed I began to push through the stone. My right foot first—it was gliding through!—and then I stopped. The rest of my leg was stuck fast, deep inside the stone.

'I moaned aloud. Over my shoulder I saw the tiger stir. I saw one eye open. Then the other. I'd forgotten the colour of those eyes: red, like coals of fire. The tiger growled deep in its throat. It made me think of the Baron, and how he would laugh to see me trapped like this. Slowly, lazily, the tiger uncurled itself.

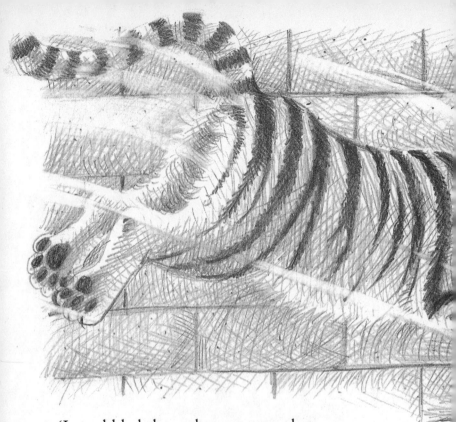

'I scrabbled through my top pockets. Nothing. I was frantic. The tiger was padding towards me. It leaned back on its haunches, ready to spring. It was hard to look away from its snarling mouth, but yes, there in the very last pocket of all, I felt something soft and squashy. Another cake crumb!

'I swallowed the crumb as the tiger sprang.
Its jaws opened and a spiky whisker swiped
my hand, but I was away, slipping through
the stone as easily as a fish noodle slips
down your throat.

'Outside it was cool and breezy, and I stretched my arms out wide and did a little dance of freedom. Then I saw Cousin Wu, coming back from his sister's. I ran to him and told him, in a great rush, what the Baron had done.

'"That thieving devil!" cried Cousin Wu. "I'd like to drop him down a great black hole, down to the burning centre of the earth! But first, let's go and tell the village."
'"You go," I said, "but just say to everyone that you've discovered who stole the hens— nothing more. There is something I have to do here first."'

'What?' cried Dad, hanging on to his
blanket.

Tashi smiled. 'I had other plans for the
Baron. You see, it was almost midnight. I
hurried down to the Baron's jetty, to wait
for the River Pirate. The moon was up, and
soon I heard the soft *shush shush* of the
motor. The boat came around the bend,
riding the moon's path of silver. The Pirate
tied up at the jetty, and stepped out.

'He was tall and looked as strong as ten
lions. I didn't fancy being taken as his
prisoner, but still I went to meet him. "I
have some news from the Baron," I began.
"He has changed his mind about selling
you the hens."

'The River Pirate frowned. It was a terrible

frown, and I noticed him stroke the handle
of his sword. Quickly I added, "But I have
something for you." I drew out of my
pocket a small bag of "gold" that a tricky
genie had given me some time ago. "The
Baron said that this is for your trouble."
'Well, the River Pirate stopped frowning,
and clapped me on the back.

'In the distance I could see a large crowd of people marching from the village. They were waving flaming torches high above their heads, shouting fiercely. And there was the Baron coming out of his house, on his way down to meet the River Pirate. He hurried over to see what all the smoke and noise was about, and when he saw me, he gasped with surprise.

'I walked up to him and said sternly, "Here come the villagers. Can you see how angry they are? How furious? You have two choices. Either I will tell them how you stole their hens—and who knows what they will do to you, with their flaming torches and fiery tempers." The Baron turned pale in the moonlight.

'"Or?" he asked. "What about the *or?*"

'"Or," I said slowly, stretching out the word like a rubbery noodle, "I can tell them you discovered that the River Pirate had stolen their hens, and, as an act of kindness, you bought the hens back for them."

'The Baron gave a great growl of relief. "That's the one I like, Tashi, my boy!"

'But I hadn't finished. "And you will invite them all to see the wonderful Flying Fireball Circus, which you will bring here to the village next week."

'"The circus? Are you mad? You sneaky little worm, that would cost me a fortune!" roared the Baron.

'"Yes," I agreed. "Don't those flames look splendid against the black sky?"

'And when the Baron turned to see, the villagers were almost upon us. "WHERE IS THE THIEF! WHERE IS THE THIEF!" they chanted.'

'And did the villagers set upon him with
their fiery tempers?' Dad asked eagerly.

'No,' Tashi smiled. 'We all went to see the
acrobats and the jugglers and the daredevil
horsemen at the circus, and we had the best
night of our lives.'

'So,' Dad sighed, 'I suppose everyone had eggs for breakfast from then on and talked about the circus over tea, and Cousin Wu saw a lot of his sister.'

'Yes,' agreed Tashi, 'life was quite peaceful—for a while. Hey, Jack,' Tashi turned to his friend, 'let's go out into the garden and play Baba Yaga.'

'Okay,' said Jack. 'I'll be the witch and you can be the dinner,' and they raced outside to the peppercorn tree.

Dad went back to bed.

and the
DEMONS

written by
Anna Fienberg
and
Barbara Fienberg
•

illustrated by
Kim Gamble

One fresh sunny morning, Jack and his
Mum were in the garden, watching Dad
plant a new gardenia bush.

'It's too *early* to be up on Sunday
morning,' Mum yawned.

But Dad couldn't wait to get his new
bush in the ground. 'Mmm,' he said,
putting his nose deep into a flower. 'That
perfume is fantastic!' He stood up, leaning
against his shovel, closing his eyes.

Jack saw an army of bull ants swarm over Dad's gumboots. Must be standing on a nest, he thought. Dad began to hop all over the pansy bed. He hit his shin with the shovel.

'Blasted things've got into my socks!'
he cried.

'Come over here,' said Mum. 'Rest a bit,
it's Sunday!'

Dad peeled off a sock while Mum lay
back in a warm patch of sun. She bunched
her dressing gown under her head.

'Ah, that's better,' she said. 'All we need
now is a story.'

'That gardenia should do well,' said
Dad, rubbing his foot. 'After all the rain
we've had, the soil is nice and moist.'

'Speaking of rain...' said Jack, settling
himself between them.

'A Tashi story, I bet!' cried Mum, sitting
up. 'What is it—floods, gushing rivers,
monster waves?'

Jack chewed a piece of grass. 'Well,
once, in Tashi's old village, it didn't rain for
months.'

'No good for *his* gardenias, eh?' said Dad.

'No,' replied Jack. 'It was no good for anything. It hadn't rained for so long that little children could hardly remember the sound of it, or the smell of wet earth. There was almost no rice left in the village, and the last of the chickens and pigs had been eaten ages ago. Every day Tashi's mother sent him a bit further to look for wild spinach or turnips or anything to add to the thin evening stew.'

'Erk!' Dad wrinkled his nose. 'Stew pew!'

'Ssh!' said Mum. 'And leave your foot alone. You'll just make it worse.'

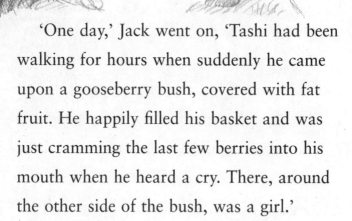

'One day,' Jack went on, 'Tashi had been walking for hours when suddenly he came upon a gooseberry bush, covered with fat fruit. He happily filled his basket and was just cramming the last few berries into his mouth when he heard a cry. There, around the other side of the bush, was a girl.'

'Berry bushes have terrible thorns,' said Dad. 'I expect she'd scratched her hands.'

'I don't think so,' said Jack. 'Tashi just said she was very pretty—sort of shiny and special, like the first evening star.'

'Oh,' said Dad. 'Gosh.'

'Go on,' said Mum breathlessly.

'Well,' Jack continued, 'Tashi saw why
the girl was sobbing. Her legs and arms
were tied up with ropes. "Who did this?
Who are you?" he asked.

'"Oh, please help me," the girl wept. "I am Princess Sarashina, and I'm the prisoner of two horrible demons. They frightened away my guards and dragged me from my travelling coach. They tied me up here two days ago and I've had nothing to eat or drink since then."

'Tashi began undoing the cords around her wrists. He noticed she was looking hungrily into his basket. But when he reluctantly offered her some berries, she said, "Oh no, not now, they might come back any minute. Where can we hide?"

'Tashi thought quickly...behind that Dragon's Blood Tree? No, it was no use hiding, he decided. He and the princess would have to come out some time, and *then* what?

'"You go back to my village," he said finally, "and I'll come later, when I find some vegetables. I'm very poor and no use to demons. They won't hurt me."

'"You never know with demons." Princess Sarashina shook her head. "My Uncle Lee says demons are like muddy water. You can never see to the heart of them and they vanish through your fingers leaving dirt on your hands. Besides, I don't know the way to your village."

'"It's easy," said Tashi. "Just follow the path between those tall trees, go past the cemetery on your right and then the temple on your left, over the bridge and there's the village. Ask for Tashi's house and tell my parents that I'll be along in a little while. As for the demons—"

'"Have you ever met one?"

'"I've seen a few in my time," said Tashi. "But never up close."

'"I hope you never do." The Princess shivered. "Their eyes are red as blood, like two whirlpools trying to suck you in. Good luck, Tashi!" And she ran off towards the trees.

'Tashi wandered through the forest, looking out for wild herbs and demons. He found some sorrel and roots and when his hands were full he decided to make his way home. He passed the gooseberry bush and was just checking to see that he hadn't left any berries—he hadn't—when suddenly he was seized by two strong arms and thrown like a ball into the air.

'He looked down into a hideous face.
The eyes were red, just as Sarashina had
said, and inside their scarlet lids the
eyeballs were swirling like flaming mud.
Tashi felt himself being drawn into them,
like a stone into quicksand. With a huge
effort he looked away, staring instead at
teeth hooking over great fleshy lips.

'"Where is Princess Sarashina? What have you done with her?" the demon bellowed. Oh, how Tashi wished he hadn't come back to the gooseberry bush!

'"I haven't done anything to her," he said firmly, just as a second demon came bounding out of the forest. But both demons were now looking hard at Tashi's jacket. There, tucked into a buttonhole, were the cords that he had untied from Sarashina's hands and feet.

'"What are these then? Where is she?" roared the first demon.

'"I won't tell."

'The second demon knocked Tashi to the ground and sat on his chest. He stared deep into Tashi's eyes, but Tashi wouldn't look back. The demon shifted angrily. Then he smiled so all his dagger teeth glinted.

'"I think you *will* tell," he said slowly.

'Tashi didn't like that smile. He thought about demons and Uncle Lee's muddy water, and how you couldn't tell what was at the bottom of it. He knew the demon had a terrible plan, but no matter how hard he tried, Tashi couldn't imagine what it might be. He started to sweat under the demon's heavy legs.

'"I think this will persuade you," the demon said, and he clicked his fingers. A box popped into his hand. "If you don't talk, I am going to tip these spiders over you." He lifted the lid a little to show Tashi what was inside.

'Tashi caught a glimpse of hairy scampering legs and quickly shut his eyes. "I will never tell."

'He pressed his lips together as he felt spiders crawling over his face and up his nose. Taking a deep breath, he tried to still his mind. Yes, that helped. Then, with a great effort, he squeezed out a giggle. "They tickle!"

'The first demon roared with rage. "Give him to me!" He pushed the other demon aside and tied Tashi to a tree with his hands above his head. "Now we'll see how you like *snakes*!"

'He muttered a demon word and a barrel of snakes appeared under the tree. Tashi quivered as snakes slithered over his legs and under his jacket. But he managed to close his eyes, relaxing his muscles and making his mind still.

'"Oh good, snakes!" he cried, grinning. "I have three snakes at home, but they're much bigger than these. I let them sleep at the foot of my bed. Snakes like the warmth, you know."

'The second demon roared with rage. "Give him back to me!" He poked the first demon's chest with a steely finger. "We will never find Princess Sarashina like this—or get the ransom you said the Emperor would pay!"

'Both demons glared at Tashi. Their eyes glowed crimson. Then they turned to each other and hissed one word: "*RATS!*"

'*Wah*, thought Tashi, I *can't* pretend with rats—sharp little yellow teeth, dripping with disease—*ugh!* He took a deep breath. "Rats don't worry me," he said loudly. "In fact, the more there are the better I like it. You can do tricks with rats, you know. Train them with a bit of cheese or meat...I do it all the time at home, with my pets Rattus and Ratz." Tashi smiled broadly at the demons. He was only able to smile, you see, because he'd just thought of a cunning demon trick.'

'That's my boy,' said Dad, looking relieved. 'I *hate* rats. We had one once in the kitchen, didn't we, Mum? It gave me nightmares and chewed my socks.'

'Well,' Jack went on, 'the demons stamped their feet and jumped about with fury.

'"Spiders and snakes and rats are really scary!" wailed the first demon. "Humans are supposed to be terrified by them." He grabbed Tashi by the jacket. "Why aren't you? What's wrong with you? What frightens *you*?"

'Tashi bit his lip and made his hands tremble. "The only thing that really scares me," he said, "is getting stuck in a Dragon's Blood Tree. Thank heavens there aren't any in these parts."

'"Ho, ho, that's where you're wrong!" whooped the demons, and they untied him in a flash and dragged him to a tree with branches so thick and twisted together that it was like a magic maze with no beginning nor end.

'"One, two, three, up!" they boomed and the demons tossed Tashi up into the tree.

'"Goodbye, Tashi!" they gloated.
"You're trapped now. No one has ever
found their way out of a Dragon's Blood
Tree, hee hee!"

'But Tashi disappeared.

'The demons waited. "Where did he go?" asked the first demon uneasily. They gazed up into the net of branches. Not even a rat could wiggle out through those. They bounded back to the gooseberry bush for a better view of the treetop. Nothing.

'"He's gone!" the demons screamed,
and they jumped into the tree to find him.
They peered and poked about, crawling
over each others' faces as they searched
for Tashi.

'Meanwhile, Tashi wriggled deeper and

deeper into the darkness of the tree. When he came to the centre of the tangled branches, he wound his way down to a hollow in the trunk. With a shiver he slipped inside. It was so black in that tunnel, and tiny soft things flitted past his cheek. The air grew musty and thick. But Tashi kept climbing down, his fingers finding rough holds. His eyes were stinging as he stared into the dark, until at last he spied a faint ray of light. Squeezing through the opening, he crawled on his belly over the roots and ran off home.

'The demons never did find their way out of the Dragon's Blood Tree, and as far as Tashi knows, they are still writhing about in the dark, roaring at each other.'

'And so what happened to the Princess, the one like the evening star?' asked Dad.

'I was just getting to that,' Jack replied. 'Princess Sarashina and Tashi's parents were almost finished their stew of dandelion roots when Tashi burst in the door. His family bombarded him with questions and the Princess was particularly interested in his demon-tricking method.

'"How did you find a way out of the Dragon's Blood Tree?" she asked him admiringly.

'"Wise-as-an-Owl told me," said Tashi. "He's taught me a million things about herbs and plants. Look for the dragon's tunnel at the centre of the trunk, he said, and follow it down till you see the light."

'Princess Sarashina was excited to hear this, and asked if Tashi could introduce her to Wise-as-an-Owl some time. Tashi agreed, and then he walked her down to the river where they found a boat to take her home.

'The next day the boat returned, laden deep in the water with bags of rice and fruit and chickens, enough food to feed the village for the summer. And with the food there was a note saying "Thank you, Tashi" from the Emperor, and an invitation from the Princess for him to visit the palace.

'That night, the villagers decorated Tashi with coloured streamers and carried him around the village on their shoulders. The feasting and laughter grew even louder as clouds blotted out the moon and the rains began to fall.'

Mum and Dad lay on the grass with their eyes closed. They didn't move. Jack looked at their faces. He prodded them.

'We're practising,' said Mum.

'We're trying to still our minds,' said Dad.

'Look, there's a bull ant!' cried Jack, and Dad leapt up as if a bee had stung him.

'Well, better be getting back to my gardenia,' said Dad. 'So when's Tashi coming over, Jack? Maybe he could give me some advice about my plants. What do you think?'

'Sure,' said Jack. 'I'll go and ring him up.'

'And I'll make him some sticky rice cakes,' said Mum. 'In just a minute,' she added, closing her eyes.

THE MAGIC BELL

'Look out, Tashi! Hide behind this tree,
quick!' Jack pulled Tashi down beside him.

'What is it?'

'Look, *there*.' Jack pointed to the
veranda of number 42. An old man leant
over the balcony. He had wild curly hair
and a cockatoo on his shoulder. He didn't
look very dangerous to Tashi. But then
Tashi had seen a lot of evil and calamitous
things in his time, it was true.

'That's Mr B. J. Curdle. He's always pestering me,' hissed Jack. 'I'm just walking home from school, right—like now, minding my own business—and out dashes old Curdle, stopping me and asking *how I am*.'

Tashi frowned. 'What's so terrible about that?'

'Well, he makes these dreadful homemade medicines from plants in his garden, and he wants to try them out on *me*! Once, I felt sorry for him—his cockatoo had a limp—so I went in. Instead of lemonade he gave me this thick yellow stuff to drink. He said it was strengthening medicine. Yuk!'

'And did it make you strong?'

'You've got to be kidding! That mixture made me weak as a baby—it tasted like mashed cockroaches. I felt like throwing up all the way home. The man's a menace!'

When the old man had gone back inside, and the two boys were walking home, Tashi said, 'What you need is a Magic Warning Bell, like the one we had in my village. It rang whenever danger was near.'

'Ooh, that *would* be handy. What did it look like?'

'Well, it was very old and beautiful, the most precious thing we had in the village. When dragons came over the mountain it would ring out, and once, when a giant wandered near, its clanging was so deafening that even people working in the fields had time to escape. Lucky for me, it rang the day the River Pirate arrived.'

Jack stopped on the path. 'Oh, I remember *him*—he was that really fierce pirate you tricked with a bag of fake gold.'

Tashi nodded. 'I had to, or I'd have been carved up like a turkey. But I always knew when he discovered it he would come back to get me.'

Jack shivered. 'So what did he do?'

'Well, it was like this,' said Tashi. 'I was in the village square getting some water from the well when the bell tolled softly. It seemed to be ringing just for me.

'I stood there, frozen, trying to think.
But all I could see in my mind was that
Pirate, stroking the end of his sword.
I sipped some water. That helped. I decided
that the first place he'd look for me would
be my house, so I dropped my bucket and
ran to my cousin Wu, who lived high up on
a hill overlooking the village.

'From Wu's front window I could see the River Pirate tying up his boat. Just the sight of him gave me the shivers. He was *huge*— the muscles in his arms were like boulders. I watched him stride along the jetty, turning into the road ... he was heading straight for my house! My mother told him she didn't know where I was, but he banged about inside anyway, frightening her and my grandparents. He knocked a pot of soup off the fire and kicked over a table, then went charging about the village asking for me.'

Jack kicked a stone ferociously. 'They'd better not tell him where you were!'

'Well, a few villagers had seen me running up to Wu's house, but they all said they had no idea where I'd gone. Still, there was one little boy who didn't understand the danger I was in. He skipped up to the River Pirate calling, "Do you want to know where Tashi is? Well—" but at that moment three large women sat on him.

'"Well *what*?" growled the River Pirate.

'"Well so do we," the women replied, and the Pirate scowled and hurried on. He searched all day, growing more and more angry. People ran into their houses and locked the doors, but he threw rocks at their windows and tore up their gardens. That night, on his way back to the boat, the River Pirate stole the Magic Bell.'

'Oh no!' cried Jack.

'Oh yes!' said Tashi. 'The next morning, when they noticed that the bell was gone, the people were very upset. The Baron told everyone that it was my fault because I had tricked the River Pirate in the first place. People began to give me hard looks. They said that the bell had hung over the well since Time began and now, because of me, the village had lost its special warning. Some little children threw stones at me and their parents looked the other way. I felt so miserable I could have just sat down in a field and never got up.

'So I went to see Wise-as-an-Owl, to ask his advice. He was busy at his workbench when I walked in, filling jars with herbs and plants.

'"Ah, Tashi," he smiled as I came in. He looked at me for a moment. "You'd better help yourself to some willowbark juice over there."'

Jack shuddered. 'What's that? Does it taste like mashed cockroaches?'

'No,' said Tashi. 'But it can cure head-aches. I've learnt everything I know about plants and potions from Wise-as-an-Owl— he's an expert on the medicine plants of the mountain and forest. So I told him yes, I would have a dose, because I *did* have a pounding headache and a terrible problem.

'Of course Wise-as-an-Owl knew all about the River Pirate. He'd watched him stamping all over his herb garden out the front. "Go and face the villain, Tashi," he told me. "It will go better if *you* find *him* first."

'He gave me two packets of special herbs to keep in my pocket. "Wolf's breath and jindaberry," he said. "Remember what I've taught you and mind how you use them."

'I thanked him and looked around for the last time at the plants and jars and pots of dandelion and juniper boiling on the stove. Then I set out for the city at the mouth of the river. There I would find the River Pirate.

'I walked for two days, and as I trudged through forests and waded through streams, I thought about what I should say to him. On the last night, lying under the stars, I decided that I'd try to make a bargain with him. What I'd offer him would be fair, and would mean a big sacrifice for me!

'I had no trouble finding the River Pirate down in the harbour. He was sitting at the end of the jetty with his black-hearted crew.

You could hear them from miles away.
They were dangling their legs over the side,
passing a bucket of beer to each other and
shouting and singing rude pirate songs at
the tops of their voices. Every now and
then they would tear great hunks of meat
from a freshly roasted pig—stolen, you
could be sure.'

'"There you are, you treacherous young devil!" the River Pirate spluttered when he saw me, leaping up and showering my face with greasy gobbets of pig. He grabbed my arm and yanked me toward him. His hand flew to his sword.

'"Wait!" I cried. "Listen!" I took a deep breath to stop my voice from trembling. Suddenly I had terrible doubts that a River Pirate could care about people being fair or making sacrifices, but it was the only idea I'd had. "If I work for you for a year and a day," I said boldly, "will you give back the bell?"

'The River Pirate just laughed. He threw back his great bony head and roared, "I will keep you for *ten* years and a day—and the bell as well!" Then the crew grabbed me and tossed me into the boat.

'By sunset we'd set sail. When the first star glittered in the sky, the cook told me to go down into the galley and start chopping mountains of fish and vegetables. And every day after that I had to do the same arm-aching jobs. The cook was spiteful and the work was hard and boring—except when it was frightening. Like the time another pirate ship attacked us.'

'*Enemy* pirates?' cried Jack. 'What did you use as a weapon—your kitchen knife?'

'Well,' said Tashi, 'it was like this. One moonless night, a swarm of bawling, yelling-for-blood pirates sprang onto our boat. They took us completely by surprise. Where could I hide? I glanced frantically around the boat and spied a big coil of rope. I scuttled over and buried myself in the rope just as the enemy Captain bounded up. He was barking orders and threats like a mad dog when he suddenly caught sight of the River Pirate. Swiping at the air with his sword, he gave a vicious battle cry—and tripped over me! *Wah!* I shivered when I looked up into his face, but he didn't hesitate for a moment. He picked me up as if I were just a weevilly old crust and flicked me overboard.

'Lucky for me there was a rope ladder hanging from the side of the boat. I grabbed it and swung down, clinging onto the last rung as I dangled in the black and icy water.

'My fingers were stiffening with cold and it was hard to hang onto the fraying strands of rope. Something slithery kept twining around my legs! I kicked hard and looked down into the dark waves. A giant octopus was staring up at me, its tentacles groping for my ankle. Then, to my horror, I felt my shoe being sucked from my foot!

'At that very moment, just when it seemed that my mother would never see her precious boy again, I heard the River Pirate and his men bellowing out their song of victory. I could hear the dreadful splash as enemy pirates were thrown over the side.

'Oh, how wet and wretched I was when I climbed back into the boat. But all I got was the River Pirate's ranting fury. "Why didn't that mangy magic bell ring to warn us?" he shouted, as he wiped the blood of an enemy pirate from his eye.

'"It only rings for the place where it belongs," I told him, and he scowled so deeply that his eyebrows met in the middle.

'The next morning, I saw three pirates racing up to the deck to be sick over the side. By afternoon two more men and the cook looked quite green. They wobbled around as if their legs were made of noodles. As our village came into sight, I said to the River Pirate, "If I can cure your men of their sickness, will you let me go?"

'"No!" snarled the Pirate, but just then he bent over and clutched his stomach.

"Aaargh, I'm dying...Go on then, but be quick," he gasped.

'I slipped down to the galley where I had hidden my packets of medicine plants. Quickly I threw some into a pot and boiled them up.

'The men only needed a few mouthfuls each before they stopped rolling about on the deck and sat up. One even smiled. The River Pirate was hanging over the side of the boat like a piece of limp seaweed, but he turned his head and begged for me to hurry.

'"And will you give me back the bell as well?" I asked him. The River Pirate ground his teeth. I tilted the pot a little. "I hope I don't spill these last few spoonfuls," I worried.

'"Ah, take the bell, take it. It doesn't work anyway," the River Pirate hissed.

'And so that's how I came back to the village with the magic bell.'

Tashi looked at Jack and laughed. 'Do you realise we've walked right past your house and mine?'

'Well,' said Jack, grinning, 'come back to my place and have a glass of lemonade. Or we could always call in on Mr Curdle if you'd prefer... But tell me, what happened when you got home?'

'The villagers all crowded around, welcoming me and saying they were sorry for their harsh words. But when I took the bell out of the sack, there was a great shout and people threw their hats in the air. We hung the bell back on its hook over the well. And then—something that had never happened before—it gave a joyful peal!'

'Gee,' said Jack, 'wasn't it lucky that the pirates got sick so that they needed your medicine!'

Tashi smiled. 'I think Wise-as-an-Owl would tell you that luck had nothing to do with it. Sometimes medicines that make you sick are almost as useful as those that make you well.'

'Aha!' said Jack, giving Tashi a knowing look, and they leapt up the steps of Jack's house, two at a time.

Tashi

and the
BIG
STINKER

written by
Anna Fienberg
and
Barbara Fienberg
•
illustrated by
Kim Gamble

'What kind of sandwiches have you got today, Tashi?' asked Jack.

'Egg,' said Tashi.

'Oh.' Jack pulled at some weeds growing under the bench. There were only ten minutes until the bell.

It was a dull kind of day, thought Jack.
The sky was grey all over. There wasn't a
single dragon or battleship or wicked face
in the clouds. And then Tashi had been
busy taking a boy to the sick bay—Angus
Figment had been bitten by a strange green
spider which made Angus's finger go all
black and dead-looking. Tashi said it
needed urgent treatment, so they hadn't
even had time to play.

'Dragon Egg.'

'What?'

'My sandwich.'

'Ooh, let me see.'

Tashi licked the last crumb from the corner of his mouth. 'Sorry, I just finished— boy, was I hungry! I could have eaten ten thousand and six of them!'

'What do dragon eggs taste like?'

'Salty, and a bit hot, like chilli—your tongue tingles as if it's on fire.'

'Gosh,' said Jack. 'I just had cheese.' He stood up gloomily.

'Once somebody really did swallow ten thousand and six of those eggs. It was terrible. Everyone said that's why there are so few dragons around any more. We were lucky—Third Aunt had already salted away piles of them, just in case.'

Jack sat down. 'In one gulp? Swallowed them, I mean.'

'Oh, sure,' said Tashi, stretching out his legs.

'Who was he? Come on, tell me, we've still got nine minutes before the bell.'

'Well,' said Tashi, throwing his lunch
scraps into the bin, 'it was like this. On a
grey, still afternoon, remarkably like this
one in fact, I was sitting with my friends in
the schoolhouse when suddenly the Magic
Warning Bell began to ring. We all ran
straight home, I can tell you! Our mothers
came in from the fields and our fathers
gathered up the animals and bolted the
doors of their shops. What danger could
there be? I wondered. Was it the war lord,
stung by wasps and gone mad? Was it
blood-thirsty pirates? Ravenous witches?

'The ground began to tremble and the dishes clattered on the shelves. Peeping through a crack in the shutters, I saw a giant striding down the street.'

'Chintu!' yelled Jack. 'Remember how
you were prisoner in his house once and
Mrs Chintu—'

'It wasn't Chintu, Jack. This giant was
almost as wide as he was tall. He swelled
out in the middle as if he had a hill under
his jumper. Well, he passed our house,
thank goodness, but he stopped next
door and do you know what? He just lifted
the roof off, as easily as you please. He
scooped up a whole pig that was roasting
on a spit and gobbled it down as he went
on his way to the end of the village.

'As soon as the earth stopped shuddering under our feet, everyone ran into the street. They were shouting with fright, telling of their wild escapes from death. "He missed me by a hair," Wu was gasping. "That great foot of his came down like a brick wall, and squashed my poor hens flat."

'"Just as well you were roasting a pig at the time, Mrs Wang," said Wise-as-an-Owl, "otherwise he might have taken you instead." A fearful groan ran through the crowd.

'"My word, yes," said Mrs Wang. "I just
heard this morning that two people have
disappeared from the village over the river."

'People were still muttering and moaning
when the village gossip ran up. Wah! That
one practically knows what you're going to
say and who you're going to visit before
you do!'

'Oh, we used to have a neighbour like
that—Mr Bigmouth. He was like the local
newspaper.'

'Well, anyway, Mrs Fo—the gossip—shouted over everyone. "My second son's wife's cousin works for Chintu the Giant, and he has just told me that Chintu's Only Brother has come to live with him. My cousin says Only Brother is a hundred times worse than Chintu. He says Only Brother eats from morning to night!" Another moan rippled through the crowd and Wise-as-an-Owl turned to me, just as I knew he would.

'"Tashi," he said, "you are the only one of us who has been to Chintu's castle and managed to leave alive. Do you think that you could go again and find out if this is true?"'

'Oh no,' said Jack. 'You didn't have to go, did you?'

'Well,' said Tashi, 'it was like this. I didn't want to, but then I thought it could be my roof that was lifted next time, and no pig in the courtyard! "All right," I said, "I'll get ready straight away."

'My mother packed some food and a warm scarf in a basket. "Be careful, Tashi," she said, "and give these plums to Mrs Chintu with my best wishes."

'I gave her a hug, and set off. It was a night and a day's hard walking ahead of me but I remembered the way well. When I arrived at Chintu's castle I stopped and listened. There was a great muttering and clanging of spoons and forks coming from the kitchen. I made my way towards it and pushed open the door. (That took a while— giants' doors are heavy!)

'There, in the kitchen, was Mrs Chintu. She was rolling some dough, her face creased with bad temper. I ran over and tugged at her skirt.

'"Well, hello, Tashi," she said, most surprised. "What are you doing here?"

'I told her about Only Brother's visit to the village and how frightened the people all were that he would come again. But when I asked if there was anything she could do to help us, Mrs Chintu threw down her chopper and cried, "I wish there was, Tashi. Only Brother is driving *me* crazy as well. He eats all day long, I never stop cooking, so fussy he is with his food. And he keeps Chintu up drinking till dawn, the both of them singing at the tops of their voices. But whenever I ask Chintu to tell him to go, he says, 'He is my Only Brother, I could never ask him to leave.'"

'Just then Chintu stamped into the kitchen roaring, "Fee fi fo—"

'"Now don't start that all over again," Mrs Chintu snapped. "Here's Tashi come to see us. You remember him, don't you? He's the boy who—"

'"Didn't we eat him?"'

'"No," said Mrs Chintu hastily, "that was another boy altogether. Is something the matter?"

'Chintu flopped down like a mountain crumbling. "You know how I've been waiting for the pomegranates to ripen on my tree down by the pond? Well, I just went there to pick some and I found that Only Brother has stripped the tree bare and eaten the lot."

'"I told you he should go," said Mrs Chintu.

'"Now don't *you* start that all over again," Chintu roared and he stamped out.

'"You see," sighed Mrs Chintu, "Only Brother will be here forever."

'"Unless we come up with a cunning scheme," I said. "Now let me think..."

'Mrs Chintu sat me on the table. "You'll think better if you're comfortable," she said.

'I closed my eyes and swung my legs and then an idea came. "Did you say Only Brother was a fussy eater?"

'"Yes, I did. Everything has to be just so, even if he does guzzle it all down in a trice."

'"Well then," I said, "for Step One, when you give him his dinner tonight, make sure that his helpings have four times as much pepper as he likes."

'At dinner time, Only Brother gulped down three or four spoonfuls of stew before he realised how hot and spicy it was. "UGH!" he bellowed. "This stew would burn the tonsils off a warthog! No giant could eat it!"

'Chintu, who had no extra pepper in his dinner, took a spoonful. "What's wrong with it?" he growled. "You probably aren't hungry because you are full of *my* pomegranates."

'The two brothers went to bed, scowling. There was no drinking or singing that night. Good, I thought, now for tomorrow—and Step Two.

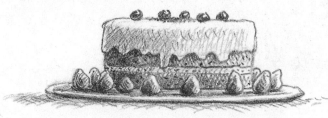

'The next morning was Chintu's birthday. Mrs Chintu spent all morning making a magnificent birthday cake. When he saw it, Chintu licked the icing on the top and said, "Now, wife, we must be sure Only Brother doesn't see this before dinnertime! I'll hide it in the cellar."

'I waited until Chintu was out of sight and then went to find Only Brother. I described the beauty of the cake and Only Brother's eyes glistened. "Would you like to see it?" I asked. "Just to look at, not to touch, of course." Only Brother would.

'We went downstairs to the cellar and Only Brother stood before the cake, mouth watering. I quietly slipped away.

'That night, after dinner and presents, Chintu went away to fetch his cake. There was a tremendous, ear-splitting roar. He came upstairs with an empty plate and a frightening scowl.

'"Oh, that," said Only Brother, shrugging his shoulders like boulders. "I meant to have just one little slice, but before I knew it, I had finished every sweet-as-heaven crumb. Mmm, delicious, delectable...ah!"

'"I've been looking forward to that cake all day!" Chintu kicked Only Brother out of the way and stomped upstairs to bed. "Only *Bother* should be his name," he hissed under his breath. Another early night.

'Good, I thought, now for tomorrow and Step Three.

'The next morning Chintu went down to the river early and stopped a fishing boat laden with lobsters, octopus and fish. He bought the whole catch and went home to tell his wife. "We will have a wonderful meal tonight—shark fin soup and seafood stew. I have left it all in a net in the river to stay cool—just tell me when you want it."

'But when Mrs Chintu sent him down to get the fish, he found Only Brother had eaten the lot—and one or two fishermen as well. Chintu shook his fist and growled.

'"Oh that," said Only Brother, shrugging his shoulders like boulders. "When Tashi told me about the fish I meant to have just one or two, but before I knew it, I had finished them all. Delicious, delectable...ah!"

'Chintu ground his teeth (it sounded like rocks crashing against each other!) and told his wife she would have to find something else for dinner. But Mrs Chintu and I were already making our preparations. I told her to tip two big sacks of beans into the cooking pot. "We'll have bean stew," I said, "and into Only Brother's bowl we'll put a few handfuls of these special berries and spices that Wise-as-an-Owl gave me."

'Only Brother liked the stew so much he had six big bowls of it. And sure enough, after a while, when he and Chintu were sitting drinking their tea, the beans did their work. "BLATT, BANG, PARF!"

'Great gusts of wind exploded from Only Brother's bottom. They were like bombs going off. And the spices we'd added to his stew made the explosions terribly, horribly smelly.

'Chintu threw open the windows and door, beetles curled over on their backs, their legs waving weakly in the air, and the canary dropped off its perch.

'Mrs Chintu ran outside, her apron over her nose. Even I was growing dizzy from trying to hold my breath, and I followed her outside.

'The smell came after us. I wiped my eyes. "How can it be so strong, Mrs Chintu?"

'"Well, Tashi, Only Brother is a giant after all, with a giant-sized bottom that makes a giant-sized smell!"

'Inside the castle Chintu was bellowing, "What a stink! What a pong! This is too much—off you go!" and he pushed his brother out the door. He galloped upstairs and gathered Only Brother's clothes and bag and threw them out the window. "Go and find someone else to keep that great stomach of yours full, why don't you!"

'"I'm glad to go," sneered Only Brother. "The food here doesn't suit me at all. Your wife uses too much pepper and her stew gives me wind. Besides," he added as he picked up his slippers, "there's a dreadful smell in your castle. You should do something about it." And he burped like a volcano erupting.

'Mrs Chintu and I did a little victory dance and then she said, "I think you had better slip away home now, Tashi. I saw Chintu giving you hard looks when Only Brother mentioned that you told him where to find the fish."

'I was only too happy to obey. But when I reached the village and tried to tell the news of Only Brother's going, no one would come out into the street.

'"We can't talk now, Tashi, there is this revolting stink. Can't you smell it? Look, even the trees are wilting!"

'"Oh, that," I said, grinning. "That's Only Brother—and it's the very reason for his leaving!"'

The bell rang out over the playground, and Jack stopped laughing. 'There's our warning to get to class,' he said. 'So, quickly, did the villagers give you a reward?'

Tashi grinned. 'No—do you know what happened? Instead of saying how brave I was to get rid of the fearsome giant, people still moan about the time I caused the terrible smell!'

Just then Angus Figment ran past. He waved, and Tashi saw that his black, dead-looking finger looked healthy again. 'It was texta,' Angus cried. 'Mrs Fitzpatrick washed it.'

Tashi laughed, and Jack blew loud exploding raspberries on his arm all the way back to class.

THE MAGIC FLUTE

'Dad,' said Jack, 'can I ask you something?'

'Sure,' said Dad. 'What's it about—turbo engines, shooting stars, hermit crabs—I'm good at all those subjects!'

'No,' Jack said, 'it's like this. Say your friend is in trouble, but when you go to save him, you hurt the person who got him into trouble. Does that mean you did the wrong thing?'

'Which friend is that, Jack?' said Dad. 'Would it be my mate Charlie over the road, or is it Henry, the one I play cards with?'

'Oh, Dad, it doesn't matter,' sighed Jack. 'It's the idea, see—a question of right or wrong. Or say you owe someone a hundred dollars and...'

'Who owes a hundred dollars?' Mum came in with three bowls and spoons.

Jack rolled his eyes. 'It doesn't matter who, Mum! Maybe I'd better tell you the whole story—just the way Tashi told me.'

'Oh boy, icecream, peaches and a Tashi story for dessert!' Dad cried gleefully.

'Yes,' said Jack sternly. 'But listen carefully, because I'll ask you some questions at the end.'

Dad leant forward, frowning thoughtfully, to show how serious he could be.

'Well,' began Jack, 'back in the old
country, it had been a good summer and
the rice had grown well. People were
looking forward to a big harvest, when a
traveller arrived with dreadful news. The
locusts were coming! In the next valley he'd
seen a great swarm of grasshoppers settle
on the fields in the morning, leaving not
one blade of grass at the end of the day.'

Dad shook his head. 'Awful damage they do, locusts. You can ask me anything about them, son. Anything. They're one of my best subjects.'

'Later,' Jack said. 'Well, the Baron called a meeting in the village square.'

'That sneaky snake!' exploded Dad. 'He diddles everyone out of their money, doesn't he!'

'That's the one,' agreed Jack. 'But now the Baron was very worried because he owned most of the fields, although everyone in the town worked a little vegetable patch or had a share in the village rice fields.

'At the meeting, Tashi's grandfather suggested hosing the crops with poison but there wasn't time to buy it. Someone else said they should cover the fields with sheets, but of course there weren't enough sheets in the whole province to do that. Tashi racked his brains for an idea but nothing came.

'Just when everyone was in despair,
a stranger stepped into the middle of the
square. He was a very odd-looking fellow,
dressed in a rainbow coloured shirt and silk
trousers. On his head was a red cap with a
bell. The people had to blink as they stared
at him—he glowed like a flame.

"'I can save your fields from the locusts," he said. Tashi looked up into his eyes. They were pale and hooded.

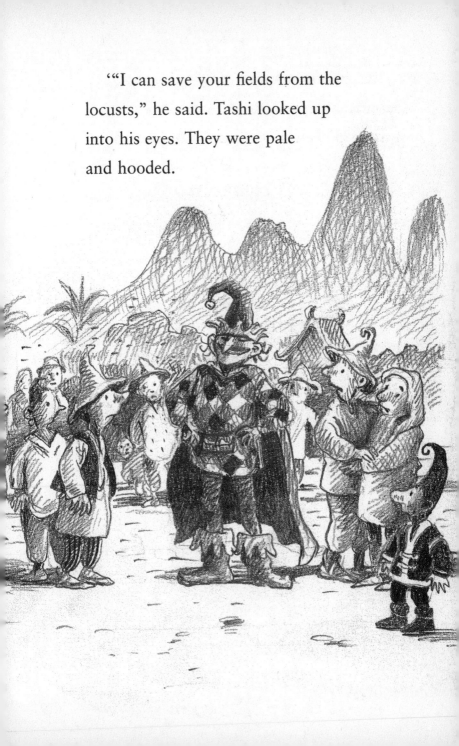

'"Can you really? How?" the people shouted as they crowded around. They wanted to believe him, and there was

something about him, this man. You could feel a kind of power that made you think he would deliver whatever he promised to do. But his eyes were full of shadows.

'"What will you need?" asked the Baron.

'"Nothing except my payment," replied the stranger. "You must give me a bag of gold when the locusts have gone."

'The people quickly agreed, and it was just as well they did. Only a moment later the sky began to grow dark and a deep thrumming like a million fingers drumming could be heard.

'Clouds of locusts appeared overhead, clouds so big and black that the sun was blocked completely, and then wah! just like that, the noise stopped and they settled on the village rice fields and gardens.

'But before the locusts could eat a blade of grass, the stranger brought out his flute and played a single piercing note. It echoed in the silence and the locusts quivered. Six shrill notes followed, and as the last note sounded, the locusts rose as one, and flew away to the south. In three minutes the air was clear.

'There was a stunned silence. People looked at each other, hardly able to believe what they had just seen. Tashi's grandfather ran up to the stranger and shook his hand, thanking him, but the Baron stepped in and cut him off. He gathered the Elders around him, saying, "Let's not be too hasty in our thanks. We can't be sure it was the stranger's flute that drove off the locusts. Maybe they would have gone of their own accord. And, in any case, a bag of gold is far too much to pay for one moment's work."

'When Tashi's father and the Elders disagreed, the Baron went on, "I know none of you has more than a few silver pieces between you, so who do you suppose would have to pay the most of it? Me, of course. Well, I won't do it, and you must all stand by me."

'Tashi felt a shiver of dread. This was the wrong thing to do. He could see that many of the others were unhappy too, and some of them started to argue with the Baron but he brushed them aside. He walked over to the stranger and tossed him a single gold coin, saying, "Here you are, fellow, you earned that coin easily enough."

'The stranger let the coin fall to the ground and slowly looked around at the people. "Do you all agree with him?"

'The people shuffled and looked away.

'"You will be sorry—oh, how very sorry," the stranger said quietly, and he drifted away, the bright flame of him shimmering in the distance.

'On the way home Tashi's grandfather took his hand and sighed.

'"We did a bad thing today, Tashi. We robbed that man of his reward."

'"Yes," said Tashi, "and I have a horrible cold feeling in my tummy telling me this is not the end of it. There was something about the way the stranger looked at us when he left. He's not an ordinary man, that's for sure."

'Tashi's family said that there was nothing they could do tonight but that in the morning they would speak with the Elders. They would find the stranger and promise to pay him, a little at a time.

'Tashi was too restless and worried to sleep. Finally he jumped out of bed and went off to see if Wise-as-an-Owl had returned yet. He had been visiting his Younger Sister who lived in the next village. Surely he would have some good advice.

'And that is why Tashi, alone of all the children in the village, never heard those first beautiful, magical notes from the stranger's flute. The children sat up in bed and listened. They ached to hear more. And soon it seemed that their veins ran with golden music, not blood, and they had to follow those notes to stay alive. Quietly they slipped from their houses and followed the music, out of the town, across the fields and into the forest.

'Next morning there were screams and cries as parents discovered that their children were missing.

'"I knew it! I knew it!" Tashi cried as he ran back into the village. Just then he spied some pumpkin seeds on the road. Hai Ping! Tashi's friend Hai Ping nibbled them all the time, and what's more he'd had a hole in his pocket lately so that he left a trail of seeds wherever he went. Without a word Tashi set off, out of the town, across the fields and into the forest.

'As the darkness of the trees closed around him, Tashi heard the faint notes of the sweetest, most lovely melody. It was like Second Cousin's finest dark chocolate dissolved into air. It made his mouth water, his ears ache, his heart pump quickly. And his fears of the stranger came flooding back. Now he knew why he'd been so uneasy about the piper. There was a story his grandmother once told him about a piper and a plague of rats. Tashi bent down and scooped up some clay to stuff into his ears. It was the hardest thing he'd ever done. He closed his eyes as the sounds of the music and forest died away.

'The pumpkin seeds had been getting harder to find and now they stopped altogether. But Tashi continued along the path, following clues he'd learned to read— a broken twig, a thread caught on a thorn bush. At last, through the trees, he saw two little boys. They were the smallest of the village children and were straggling behind. They mouthed something which Tashi couldn't hear, and pointed up ahead.

'Tashi saw the other children nearing the top of the hill. Suddenly he realised where they were all heading and his blood froze. The path ended in a sheer drop, down, down, a hundred metres down to the rushing waters of a mountain gorge. The piper was playing the flute while the children streamed past him—towards the cliff. He was playing them to their deaths! Wah!

'Tashi raced up and burst out of the bushes. He butted the piper over, knocking the flute out of his hands. The children stopped, their eyes no longer blank, their minds no longer bewitched. Slowly they gathered around as Tashi and the stranger struggled towards the edge of the drop.

'"The piper was leading you over this cliff!" Tashi gasped. The children formed a wall and closed in on the piper.

'With a desperate pull, Tashi broke free from the stranger and rolled away towards the flute, which was lying half-hidden in the grass. He picked it up and hurled it with all his strength out over the cliff edge.

'The stranger gave a groan of rage but Tashi cried, "It wasn't the children's fault that you weren't paid. You had better go quickly before our parents come."

'The stranger looked up at the stony faces of the children and he shrugged. They moved aside to let him pass and all watched silently as he disappeared into the forest.

'The children met the search party of parents on the way back to the village and they told them what had happened. Some parents wept, and they looked at each other with shame.

'"Just think," they said, "but for Tashi, we would have been too late."

'The Baron kept very busy away from the village for the next few weeks and when he did finally return, he looked rather guilty and was so polite that people thought he must be sickening for something. But he was soon back to tricking people out of their wages and charging too much for his watermelons again, so life went on as before.'

'Blasted Baron!' cried Dad.
'He's got the morals
of a dung beetle!'

'Worse. Dung beetles do some very good work,' put in Mum.

'But don't you see,' said Jack. 'It wasn't right that the piper never got paid—'

'But he was about to do a very dreadful thing!'

'But if he hadn't been treated badly in the first place—'

'Well,' said Mum, clearing away the dishes, 'people have been discussing what's right and wrong for centuries—and we've only got half an hour before *The Magic Pudding*'s on.'

'Yeah,' agreed Dad. 'Why don't you ask me about turbo engines—they don't take so long, and they take you far!'

Jack grinned. 'The day Tashi found a pair of magic shoes, he travelled 100 kilometres in one leap!'

'No, really?' cried Dad. Then his face dropped. 'But I bet that's another story, right?'

'Right,' laughed Jack. 'And now, Dad, the clock's ticking. What would you have done if *you* were the piper?'